Plastic Monsters

Daniel J. Volpe

Cover design by: Don Noble
Edited by: Patrick C. Harrison III
Printed in the United States of America

For Donna Latham...my number one fan.
PS + AW

Plastic

Monsters

"Do you want to be beautiful?"
"Yes, more than you know."
"What are you willing to pay?"
"Everything."
"What are you willing to do?"
"Anything."

Part 1: Beauty is...

January 7th 2002

Holding her sagging breasts, Pamela Rose stood in front of the mirror, and wept. The tile floor of the locker room was cool, but her blood was boiling. Her hair, a shade of dirty blonde that other girls, *the cunts*, referred to as 'trashy blonde', was wet and dripping. There was no more talking, no more laughing; they were gone. At least for the time being. It didn't matter. She still had five months left with them. Five months until her senior year was over and she could move on, leaving this shit hole small town behind.

They had left the locker room, but their insults remained.

Pam hated showering after gym; no, she fucking loathed it. For whatever reason, her school made it mandatory. It probably had to do with the staff infections amongst the freshmen boys, who were notoriously disgusting. Whatever the reasoning, the school and the parents agreed: good hygiene wasn't a laughing matter. So, everyone, even the senior girls, had to shower after every PE class. It wasn't the worst thing in the world, but it was a pain in the ass for sure. The school had individual stalls, which were narrow, but private. Some of the girls—the pretty girls, the girls with perky, firm tits—would parade around naked. They didn't care who saw. In fact, they *wanted* the other girls to look. To watch them strut around with ski slope tits and little round asses. Even a few of the more well-endowed girls would walk nude. Their breasts, for the size of them, barely hung. Ah, the gift of youth. Well, it was a gift for some, but not Pam. Her breasts were far from large, but they were heavy. She had a decent body; tight, athletic, but with a little leftover baby fat. Nothing major and nothing that kept the boys away. But her breasts, the bane of her existence. They hung like those of an old woman, and weren't even that attractive, at least in her eyes.

She would go out of her way to not let anyone see them, especially *the cunts*. But even more so Ashley Rogers, the queen of *the cunts*. Ashley was a girl that every girl hated, but wanted to be. Average height, highlighted brown hair, athletically gifted, well-off family and above all, a smoking body. She was a dainty girl, but her breasts were larger than they should be. Bordering on C-cups, they stood at attention, with just the slightest upturn. Even her nipples were cute and small, ringed with just the lightest pink areolas. The girls wanted to be her and the boys wanted to fuck her. Pam just fucking hated her.

No, Pam loathed her. She always had, ever since elementary school. Ashley was the kind of girl that would trip you, kick dirt in your face and then, with the sweetest smile, ask if you were okay. She made her living off of other people's grief. It was like sustenance for her and the rest of *the cunts.*

Over the years, Pam was able to avoid her, but it wasn't always possible. Softball was the driving force. Pam was good, and she knew it. Ashley, one of their top pitchers, was also good. So, as much as she wished otherwise, the girls were forced together.

Pam and the rest of the girls had finished up an uneventful PE class. It wasn't the best, especially just returning from Christmas break. She was changing in the locker room, waiting for a shower stall to open up. It was a normal scene: cliques of girls around lockers, chatting about their break, what they did, what they got. Pam's best friend and really only friend, Amanda, had PE later in the day. So, Pam sat with her shower stuff ready to go. She heard the water turn off at one of the closest stalls and stood up. No one else was making a mad dash to the shower, so she walked over and waited.

The curtain flew open and there stood Ashley, nude and glistening. She had a towel pressed to her face, hanging down to partially cover her breasts.

Pam looked her up and down; she couldn't

help it. The perfection of her chest, the toned stomach, the cute, trimmed pubic hair…it was all perfection. It was all she'd wanted. For a moment, a vision flashed into Pam's mind: Ashley ugly. No more symmetrical face, but one that was lumpy and awkward. No perfect set of tits, but ones that were mismatched, drooping and full of stretch marks and veins. A wild bush, with disgusting, brown pussy lips. There was something else Pam saw too: blood. She imagined Ashley bloodied. Her teeth shattered, nose broken and eyes blackened…

"What the fuck are you staring at, you fucking dyke?" Ashley's shrill voice echoed off the tiles in the locker room. Conversations stopped and everyone looked to their queen.

Pam snapped out of her daydream, realizing it was her that was being talked to. Her mind raced and her skin went cold.

"Oh, sorry, I was looking past you in the stall. Just making sure no one else was heading in." It was a weak lie, but it was better than saying *I was thinking about what you'd look like beaten and bloody.*

Ashley laughed her off, but there was something evil lurking in her brown eyes. "Huh, yeah sure." She threw the towel around her shoulders, exposing her entire nude body. "Listen, if you're a softball dyke, that's okay. I know how I look." She struck a few poses and garnered a few catcalls from some of the other *cunts*. "But," she leaned in close, the smell of her conditioner strong in Pam's face, "this pussy is for boys only. No carpet munchers, okay?"

Pam's hand itched. She didn't know why, but it did. It itched and begged. Begged her to use the nails to gouge Ashley's face. Or maybe a quick headbutt, shattering that nose. She didn't do it though, only nodding instead. The urge lingered. The urge called to her to destroy something beautiful.

"Got it," Pam squeaked.

Ashley brushed past her, into the throng of other girls.

Pam entered the steamy shower. A small bench and two hooks were on one side. They were semi dry, but better than nothing. She could hear the others talking, but it was mundane stuff and not about her. Thankfully. Quickly, she undressed, and turned on the water. Pam stayed away from the spray until she knew it was warm enough to enter. She didn't want to get her hair wet, but forgot her shower cap. Some girls could seemingly dodge the water, keeping their hair dry, but Pam never could. She accepted the inevitable and entered the spray. Through the sound of water splashing over her, she never heard the slap of bare feet on the tile just outside of her stall.

"Let me see if I left it in here," Ashley said, ripping the curtain to Pam's shower open wide.

Pam thought she was having a nightmare. The sound of the rings sliding on the shower curtain were like nails on a chalkboard. She spun in abject horror, nude and wet, looking at the queen of *the cunts*.

Ashley stood in a bra and panties (matching, of course) with her hair wrapped in a towel. She looked Pam up and down with an evil smile rising on her lips.

"Ugh, what the fuck's up with your tits?" Ashley asked, pointing at Pam's nudity.

The other girls, hearing their leader shout, quickly made their way over to see what the commotion was about.

"Fuck, I've seen some udders before, but Pam might be an old Bessie," laughed Ashley. She was pointing now, as if there was any doubt of what she was looking at.

Marley, Ashley's second in command, slid in next to her friend. "Oh my god, look at her fucking bush." She directed her eyes to the thatch of thick, black pubic hair between Pam's legs. "Ah, it's called a razor, Pammy. God, no wonder no one will fuck her." Marley looked at her with a disgust.

Pam was hot, red hot with anger and shame. She tried to cover her chest and her crotch at the same time, but it was a losing battle. Reluctantly, she tried to cover both breasts with one arm and use her free hand to cover her vagina.

When her left breast popped free, *the cunts* howled like a band of hyenas.

"Fucking gross."

"My grandmother has better tits than that."

"What's with the stretch marks? Did this

cow have a calf?"

Pam's rage overcame her shame and she rushed forward, grabbing the curtain. She pulled it, but Ashley held it tight.

"Let it fucking go," Pam said, her voice quivering with tears.

"Or else what?" Ashley asked, the air of superiority thick in her voice.

Something cracked in Pam. It didn't quite break, but the thoughts of violence, of seeing Ashley's face shattered, of seeing her dead on the ground, came rushing back.

"Or else I'll fucking kill you," Pam growled. The threat coming from anyone else would've sounded thin veiled and weak. But not from Pam. The rage and fury in her eyes told it all. She looked at each of them, cutting off their laughter with a glare.

Ashley swallowed and let go of the curtain. "I'm done looking anyway. If I want to see gross pigs, I'll go to a farm."

Pam ripped the curtain closed, nearly tearing it from the rail. Her heart was racing, but she stood ready for another attack. None came and moments later, she felt the draft of the door opening. She walked out of the shower, not bothering to even clean herself. Her towel was in her hand, but she knew she was alone. Pam walked nude to the closest mirror...and wept.

Victoria Rose stared at her daughter, who was picking at a slice of frozen pizza. She would never think of eating such trash, but Pam had always been a picky eater. Besides, she was old enough to make her own decisions. If Pam didn't care about her body, why should she?

Pam dropped the crust of the pizza and looked up at her mother, who was staring at her.

Vicky almost sneered at the piece of the tomato caught in her daughter's teeth. She set her fork down, resting it on her mostly uneaten salad. Pam was her opposite: short, darker hair, oily skin, and still carrying around baby fat. Even though the girl played softball, her diet and lack of care for her body negated anything she did. Vicky, hovering just under forty-years old, was tall, thin, toned and had the smooth skin of a baby's ass.

"Mom, how can I make my skin," Pam paused, hoping she didn't come across as crazy. Who was she kidding, beauty was no laughing matter to her mother? "Tighter?"

Vicky looked at Pam, that look of judgement. The glaring eye, the stare of knowing you're beneath her. It was the look Vicky cast on many women, even her daughter.

"Well, first and foremost, stop eating like a pig," Vicky said, a plastic smile on her face.

Pam's slight grin fell hard and she looked at the crust on her plate.

"Oh, stop it, Pamela. You know what I mean. You eat like you're still six, not seventeen. And look at what it's doing to you. Your skin, your weight, your hair? A little skin tightening isn't going to work miracles, Pam."

The tears were stinging Pam's eyes. She didn't know what to expect from her mother, but she was far from shocked. Vicky never missed a chance to take a shot at Pam, often times reminding her of her modeling career that went up in smoke the day she found out she was pregnant. The father left the day after fucking Vicky when her photo shoot was over.

Vicky could see the hurt on her daughter's face. A part of her, a hidden, motherly part, almost felt bad. *Almost.*

"Listen," she said, hoping to end this conversation quickly. *Wheel* was coming on soon and she didn't want to miss it. "Start your day with a cold shower, okay? It sucks, but beauty is pain and pain is beauty."

Pam looked at her, rubbing the back of her hand over her red eyes. She didn't speak, but nodded.

"Great, good talk," Vicky said, standing. She pointed to the dishes on the table and the mess on the counter. "Clean this up. I'll be in the living room." She sauntered away, giving her daughter a look at a perfect behind.

Pam sat there, staring at nothing. The fractured part of her psyche, the part injured by *the cunts*, cracked just a little more.

At some point during her shows, Vicky heard the backdoor open and close. When the last gameshow host had signed off for the night, she realized she hadn't heard the door open again. Vicky turned the TV off, listening.

"Pam?" she called out, waiting to hear her daughter respond. Nothing. Near silence. The only sound was the frigid January wind buffeting the house. Vicky shivered at the sound of the icy gusts. Just the thought of being outside made her cold. "Pam?" she called again, this time getting up from the couch. Vicky wandered into the kitchen, seeing the dishes sitting on the table and counter. Her heart began to race, fearing the worst.

The backdoor was shut, but there was no trace of her daughter. Vicky flipped on the outside lights, illuminating the backyard.

Snow blew in the wind, cutting across the light like lasers. Something was on the ground. It fluttered at the next gust and Vicky knew what it was. Pam's shirt.

"Pam!" Vicky yelled, pulling the door wide open. The arctic breeze stung her eyes as she walked into the snow only wearing her slippers.

More clothes lay scattered and windblown across the yard. Something lay just at the fringes of the reach of the light. Something long and pale…and not moving.

Vicky ran into the cold, racing towards her daughter.

Pam lay nude in the snow, staring up at the night sky, her skin nearly white, and her lips blue. Her nipples and areolas were shriveled and puckered.

"Pam!" Vicky yelled, standing over her daughter. "What the fuck are you doing? Are you okay?"

Pam stared at her mother, looking up at her. Always looking up at her. With blue lips, she smiled. Her lips were cracked from the cold, and just the slightest bit of blood oozed from them.

"Am I pretty now, Mommy?" Pam's smile widened and widened, until it reached the limits of her flesh. And then…she laughed.

Chapter 1

Present Day

Holding her sagging breasts, Pamela Rose stood in front of the mirror, and wept. She took a deep, shuddering breath, willing the tears away. Her eyes were already puffy and she'd run out of rejuvenation cream the night before. The last thing she needed was for her eyes to look swollen and red before work. That wasn't acceptable. Her tits she could support and cover, but her eyes were there for everyone to see.

Pam let her breasts hang. Her nipples were hard, centered on puckered areolas. She had ended her shower with a burst of cold water, which she'd read was supposed to tighten skin. She'd yet to see any results other than hard nipples and shivering.

The mirror was full-length and free-standing. It was one of the nicest things in her small apartment, even though it was second hand. She wiped her eyes with the backs of her hands, thankful she'd chased the tears away. Her reflection looked back at her, judging.

Pam put her hands on her hips, which seemed to widen each and every day. She turned slightly, giving a look at her ass. The cellulite wasn't much, but it was there. To her, her ass looked like the surface of the moon. Regardless of how many squats she did, there was no way to bust the lumps from her butt. Unless she sprung for plastic surgery, which wasn't quite in her budget.

She faced the mirror straight on again. Her stomach was nearly flat, but her 38-year-old skin wasn't as tight as it had been in high school. Another sin in her eyes. She looked down at her vagina, which was trimmed and waxed to a perfect, and classy 'V' of pubic hair. It hadn't seen any action (besides a vibrator) in a while, but she couldn't stand a messy snatch.

Each second she looked at her reflection was an eternity. Each glance found a new dimple, red mark or loose skin. The stinging in her eyes was returning and she needed to get the fuck away from the mirror before she broke down.

Pam's cellphone dinged and she grabbed it from the bed. Her delivery of products was only three stops from her apartment.

"Thank fucking God," she muttered, and set the phone back down. Pam put on her robe, covering her nudity. Now she wouldn't have to go to work without really putting on her face.

She became obsessed with all-natural make-up, but not for moral reasons. No, if there were an abundance of dyes or chemicals, she'd break out. Her skin couldn't handle much change and even a slight hiccup could make her skin revert to teenage years. That *was not* ok.

But, first things first. Pam needed to dry her damp hair.

She walked into her small bathroom and turned on the light. Another imperfect reflection stared back at her. She pushed them from her forebrain, knowing her serums and coverups would soon be dispelling all of them. Banishing them under a thin blanket of powder and gel. Pam grabbed her blow dryer and brush and went to work.

Her hair was in a frenzy as the cool air blew over it. The *cool* setting on the blow dryer was almost as uncomfortable as the cold shower, but heat dried her skin, which led to premature wrinkles, another deadly sin.

The doorbell rang, which she barely heard over the sound of the appliance. She was almost done, but the urge to leave and grab the package was overwhelming. Finally, her hair was dry, at least dry enough. She tossed everything on the sink and briskly walked to the door, feeling her body jiggle.

Pam opened the door and grabbed the package. It wasn't much, but cost her almost half a paycheck. A small price to pay for beauty, that was certain. Each and every day, she felt her age. Luckily, there were products to counteract it, at least she believed.

With a smile on her face, she pushed the door shut and took her box into the kitchen. She threw open the junk drawer and removed an old box cutter. Gently, as not to disturb the product inside, she sliced the tape. She tossed the box cutter on the counter before digging in.

A note, a generic postcard from the company, rested atop a nest of shredded paper. Pam ripped through the packaging, revealing a small collection of little jars and tubes. Mere ounces of product, but worth its weight in gold, as far as Pam was concerned. She clutched the box to her chest, like it contained a cure for an illness. An illness besides vanity.

Pam spread out her collection on the counter, her near breakdown all but forgotten. With a practiced hand, she prepared herself for work.

Pam hated riding the bus, but there was no way she could afford a car. On her salary, she was lucky to have an apartment, let alone a reliable vehicle. It didn't matter, seeing as she didn't go out much anyway. Everything she needed was within walking distance of her apartment and the bus schedule was pretty vast. Besides, a car payment would cut into her beauty supplies, and that wasn't going to happen.

The 8:30 am bus was packed, which was normal. Pam had found a seat next to another woman, who was not nearly as attractive as her. Her seatmate was dumpy looking. She wore an old long sleeve shirt with some stupid fucking cartoon on it. Her hair was in a ponytail full of bumps and split ends. Even her jeans were unflattering and high, probably covering a stomach loose from giving birth.

Pam sat next to her with a smile on her face, knowing she was more put together, more attractive, more stylish and certainly smelled better. Anyone walking on the bus would be able to see that. Her skirt was professionally cut, with a pair of nude stockings keeping her legs tight. Her blouse was snug against her chest, accentuating the padded bra, but loose in the mid-section

The bus rumbled through the city, seemingly hitting every pothole known to man. Pam pulled a small compact from her purse, a Michael Kors bag that cost more than three months' rent, and checked her makeup. It was flawless, but a new wrinkle, one by the corner of her mouth, seemed to deepen every day. She was wearing a pretty bold lip stain, which would hopefully distract anyone from looking at the crease on her face. Pam angled the mirror up, making sure any of the puffiness and redness was gone from her eyes. Her brown eyes were clear and every last trace of distress was gone from them.

The brakes of the bus squealed as it slowed in front of her stop.

Pam pursed her lips and snapped the compact shut. The woman next to her, who seemed to be dozing off, jumped at the sound.

"Oh, sorry," Pam smirked as she shouldered her purse, slipping the mirror into the bag, "I didn't mean to startle you."

The woman, whose eyes were red, offered up a weak smile.

"No problem. I can't fall asleep anyway or I'll miss my stop." She yawned, stifling it with her hand.

Pam nearly cringed seeing the woman's unmanicured fingernails. They even looked chewed.

"Right," Pam said, holding on to the seat as the bus lurched to a halt. The aisle began to fill with passengers and she fell in line.

"Have a good day," the dumpy woman said.

Pam was silent, her confidence level at 1000, as she followed the crowd off the bus and onto the street.

Her day had gone from bad, to good, to great. She didn't know it was about to go to shit.

Pierce and Bateman employed nearly one hundred people and Pam was one of them. Most of the employees were low-level and primarily there for data entry. Pam hated her job, but with her lack of discernable skills, she was lucky to have solid employment. The job was mundane and could probably be accomplished from home, but Mr. Rosamilia wouldn't have it.

It wasn't hard to see why; almost all of the employees were women and most were quite attractive.

Pam didn't like the job, but a glance from her boss, or a sneer from one of the fatter, less put together women made her day. But she was far from the top in the realm of looks and physique.

Pam watched the numbers on the elevator rise, until it stopped at her floor. With a *ding* the doors parted.

The office was typical: rows of cubicles, a few strategically placed water coolers, a small dining area, and a couple of offices.

Faces peeked out from cubicles like meerkats scanning for a predator. Women perked up, looking at Pam, the disappointment on their faces.

Pam was a little taken aback. Usually no one cared who walked through the elevator, unless it was the delivery guy. Pam, feeling the sting of their sneers, held her head high and strutted to her cubicle.

She was looking good and she knew it. The hiccup in front of the mirror was in the past, and she lived in the present. She couldn't stand to think of the future; of aging. Drying up like a withered old hag. No, she would do anything to stay young and beautiful.

Pam took her purse from her shoulder and set it down on her desk. Her inbox was full of paper, which was typical for a Monday morning.

Tamara, one of the few women Pam was actually friendly with, was walking by.

"Hey, Tams," Pam said, stopping her mid-stride.

Tamara was in the same boat as Pam. Both mid-30s, single, but still with a bit of their youthful looks. Tamara wasn't as pretty as Pam, but that was a given.

"Yeah?" Tamara asked, brushing a loose strand of hair from her forehead.

"What's all the hubbub about?" Pam looked down the aisle as more of the women were chatting in little clusters.

"You didn't hear?" Tamara asked in a matter-of-fact tone.

Pamela didn't respond, just shrugged. Clearly, she didn't hear, or else she wouldn't be asking.

"Denise is coming back today."

Pam's smile, the one that was causing so many creases in her skin, wavered. A feeling of dread—slow, creeping dread—washed over her.

"I—I thought she was done?" Pam asked, willing her voice not to waver.

Tamara put her hand on her hips, which

were wider than Pam's and said, "Yeah, apparently she's not. That was a little rumor Mr. Rosamilia started, so he could protect his queen bitch." She held the last syllable, drawing it out.

Pam was suddenly warm. The office was always kept chilly (supposedly for the computers, but the hard nipples were a plus for the boss), but Pam felt like it was a summer day. Her light blue blouse didn't seem like such a good idea. Nothing helped start a Monday like walking around with pit-stains the entire day. Panic. Panic was returning. She felt like she was in front of the mirror again, but this time it was worse. It was almost to the level of panic she'd felt in high school. Not quite, but borderline.

"Denise was out alright, but it was for a little *procedure*," Tamara spat. Her head snapped towards the elevator, which was coming up towards them.

Pam wanted to claw at her collar. She couldn't breathe. Fuck sweating, she couldn't breathe.

Tamara was looking away. Her eyes, and the eyes of the rest of the women watched and waited.

Pam grabbed her water bottle from her desk and sipped. It was old, left-over from Friday, but she needed something. The lukewarm water helped her catch her breath, but the *dinging* on the elevator was like a countdown to destruction.

"What procedure did she have?" Pam felt herself asking. She didn't have to ask; she already knew.

Tamara looked at her side-eyed, focusing on the elevator. "What do you think? Little Miss Flat Chest had her hubby buy her a set of tits, or so I've heard."

Pam kept her panic under control, willing the beast inside of her to be still. It was calm for the moment, but she could feel it writhing in her gut.

"Probably a couple shots of Botox too," Pam said, her full attention back on the elevator. "Fucking skank."

Finally, the elevator stopped, and opened.

Denise Perkins stood there as the doors spread for her. She looked around, not stepping out of the car, but surveying her domain. She was young, perhaps the youngest at Pierce and Bateman, but she had an air of superiority reserved for gorgeous youth. The doors quivered and she stepped, timing her exit perfectly.

When teenage boys created their dream girl, they drew pictures of Denise Perkins. She was tall, but didn't look spindly. In fact, she had a model look about her, but not a starving model. Denise was thin, but she still had curves where it counted. Her behind was a thing of beauty, perfectly round and no droop. The symmetry of her face was near perfect, and her nose had just the slightest up-turn to it. Blue eyes and auburn hair framed a face of tan skin. If there was one thing missing from making Denise into a goddess, it was a pair of tits. She wasn't flat chested, but what she did have wasn't much. It didn't fit her body, that was for sure. It was the one thing that kept her down on the level with most of the other women. Until now.

Denise wore a loose jacket, which covered her chest, but stopped right above her ass. She'd never cover that.

"Ah, my star employee has returned," Mr. Rosamilia said, appearing from his office, as if his pervert radar alerted him. He almost opened his arms for a hug, but his last hug on an employee landed him in hot water with Human Resources.

Denise smiled at him; her cold eyes stopped him in his tracks.

"I'm happy to be back," she said, taking her gaze off him and looking around the room.

The rest of the women were trying their hardest to not stare, but they were all waiting for the same thing: for her to take off the damn jacket.

"It seems a little warm in here," Denise said, fanning herself with a perfectly manicured hand.

Pam looked at her own fingers. Yes, she had her nails done the day before, but the quality of Denise's fingers were evident, even from across the room.

Denise unsnapped her top button with those expensive fingers, working each one in turn. She pulled the jacket open, stripping it off.

Yup, she'd had her tits done and done big.

Denise wore a gray dress that looked more suited for a cocktail lounge as opposed to an office.

It was snug everywhere, accentuating not only her new breasts, but the flatness of her stomach. The top was near to bursting. She'd gone up a solid 2 cup sizes in her bust.

The room gasped and then grumbled. The show was over and the rest of the women went back to work, wallowing in their insecurities.

"Fucking bitch," Tamara sneered, watching Denise make her rounds, saying hi to everyone.

Pam didn't look, nor did she say anything to her friend as she walked away. She was on the verge of tears again.

Why did she have to get tits? Why? Pam asked herself, pulling the first piece of paper from her rack. *Maybe a little tummy tuck, or Botox in her face. But, tits? It made her perfect.*

Pam's mind raced back to only a few hours prior. The sting of the tears as she looked at her aging breasts, drooping and puckered in the mirror. They weren't even that great when she was young, but age had taken its toll on them. She even tried her face-firming cream on her chest, but nothing except surgery could remedy her ailment. Pam had a better chance of going to the moon than getting a boob job.

The smell of *Joy Baccarat* wafted into her cubicle. Only one person in the building could afford a $2000 bottle of perfume.

Pam wished her phone would ring at that moment. She wished her computer would fucking light on fire, she didn't care. The last thing she wanted was to talk to Denise, but it seemed inevitable. Slowly, as if surprised by her presence, Pam turned her head.

"Denise," she said with a fake smile plastered on her face.

"Pammy," Denise nearly shrieked as she opened her arms, beckoning her coworker to her.

Pam stood, adjusted her skirt and moved in to hug Denise.

Denise wrapped her tight, pressing Pam against her new, perfect breasts.

Pam hugged her back, nearly crying on her expensive dress. The feeling of Denise's chest against hers was agony. Cruel torture.

The letter opener. It's sharp, at least the tip. I wonder what would happen if I stuck her in the tits with that? Would they pop? Would they just weep expensive fluid, mixed with blood?

Pam's heartbeat felt out of whack; the thoughts of maiming Denise had her aflutter. Flashes of *the cunts* in high school lit up her memory. The ideas of what she wanted to do to them; all of them. And then, she remembered what she'd done to Ashley's face. *That* memory was a good one, yes indeed, but it wasn't enough to blot out the torment of her school life.

"How nice to see you," Denise said, releasing the embrace. Her point was across. She looked Pam up and down, making mental notes of everything she had on.

"You too," Pam said, her plastic smile

holding strong.

My God, they feel even better than they look, Pam thought. The phantom touch of Denise lingered on her body. She could feel the suppleness of her fake tits through her clothes, into her skin. *I bet they hang naturally too. Not too high, not too low, just fucking right. The Goldilocks of tits.* Pam's smile was beginning to hurt and she let it waver, afraid of the extra lines it would cause.

"I thought you had left. Moved on to greener pastures."

Denise waved her off. "No, I love working here too much." She opened her arms to display the room around her, as if they were in a mansion and not a plain office building. "Besides, Bradley says I need a job to keep me occupied and this one suits me just fine." She leaned in close, getting her plump lips almost against Pam's ear.

Pam didn't move, letting the other woman come to her. It was petty, but she needed a little victory.

"He thinks I'll fuck someone else," Denise whispered, with a small, child-like giggle on the end of it. "Trust me, he fucks me plenty...and damn good too."

Pam broke out in goosebumps at the sweet breath tickling her ear. A warmth, this not of anger, but of lust, ran through her body. She hadn't had sex, let alone *good* sex, in quite a while. The thought of Denise's tight, young husband pounding away on her made her ache.

"But," Denise backed away, "I like working here." She looked back towards the elevator, where Mr. Rosamilia was talking to one of the other women. "Especially since HR scared him straight." She looked Pam in the face, her eyes narrowing.

Pam could feel her gaze, her judging gaze on her flesh. It almost bore into her. She wanted to reach up and rub her face, to wipe off whatever imperfection that youthful goddess had spotted.

"What's the matter?" Pam asked, the overwhelming urge of judgment making her heart flutter. She caught a few other women watching the small exchange.

Denise's smile flicked back to her face and all seemed forgotten. "Oh, nothing." There was obviously something, but part of her liked watching Pam squirm. It wasn't a conscious thought, more of an ancient, deep-seeded feeling of pleasure. To put someone else down to lift yourself up. It was subconscious, but lived in every person. And to the beautiful or rich, it seemed to thrive. To beg to be able to play with the less than desirable. The peasants of the world, who had neither beauty nor money.

"What, what?" Pam grabbed her purse, which seemed cheap next to Denise. She removed her compact and looked at her face. Her makeup was still good, nothing hanging from her nose, so what could the other woman be looking at?

Denise put a condescending hand on the older woman's shoulder. "Did you have a late night? Your eyes look a little puffy."

Pam felt like she'd been struck by lightning. Her heart seized, as if it was wrapped in an iron fist. She tried to find words, but was afraid her voice would betray her. She'd either break down in tears or shout obscenities in Denise's face. But it wouldn't stop there, no. Once the dam broke there was no way to put the water back in. She would scream and yell, but then she'd attack. She'd tackle Denise to the ground, pulling clumps of her hair at the root. Her manicured nails would dig rents in the smooth, tan skin. Her moisturized knuckles would flatten her nose and blacken her eyes. But would she stop there? She didn't know. The scissors, the letter opener, the fucking stapler? They were all so close, so shiny, so fucking deadly.

Pam was so lost in her reverie, she didn't notice Denise holding something.

"Here," Denise said, offering her a small jar. "I use this before bed if it's a late night."

Pam's body was on auto-pilot, as she watched her hand, which felt like a phantom limb, take the jar. Her eyes, keen on brands, realized the small jar had cost more than her entire last shipment of beauty supplies.

Pam's tortured mouth shifted, her lips rising as she glared at the jar of cream. She looked at Denise, who was staring at her.

"Thanks," Pam muttered, wishing Denise would leave her alone. "I'll give it a shot." The words tumbled without grace.

I would give my last cent in the world to smash this jar into your fucking face. To take the fucking shards and stick them up your perfect, tight ass. There was a tic in her eye that was creeping up, but Pam blinked hard, willing it away.

"Anyway, let me get to work. Maybe we can grab lunch?" Denise asked, not knowing the woman in front of her was daydreaming horrific things.

Pam knew there was no way in fucking hell she would be having lunch with this woman. "Sure thing, as long as I can bust through this stack." She looked back at her inbox, which seemed to never end.

"Great. See you soon, Pammy," Denise said, with just a little venom on her tongue.

They hugged again, this time not as long. The message had been sent.

Pam collapsed into her chair, feeling like she'd just gone through a traumatic experience. Her mind was racing, playing back the conversation on repeat. The subtle jabs, the flexing of wealth, the fact Denise used this job as a little hobby, so her husband didn't think she was fucking anyone else.

Pam leaned over and looked at her computer. She had a lot of work to do and needed to get started. She couldn't stand falling behind and it was the last thing she wanted at the beginning of her week.

She rested her chin in hand, watching the

old machine start up, when she heard her phone go off. Not many people messaged her, so she was a little taken aback.

Pam grabbed her phone from her purse and saw it was Kelsie.

'Hey, I grabbed a 50 unit. U good today?' the text message read.

Pam felt like she was on a rollercoaster of a day and it was only 9:15 am. Her fingers flew over the screen and a little smile crept over her face.

'Sure am. Your place?' she replied.

'Yup, 730 good?'

'See you then.' Pam felt a wave of relief wash over her. Fuck Denise's magical, expensive cream, she was getting something better: Botox.

Chapter 2

Pam winced as the needle went into her forehead. It wasn't a new sensation, but she was far from comfortable.

Kelsie was almost face-to-face with her, but she had to be sure of her injection sites. One bad shot could be a disaster. It wasn't a problem in the doctor's office, where she had actual surgical lighting, but in her garage, things were different. She pulled the needle out.

"Ok, that was thirty units in your forehead. I can do ten in each eye or around your mouth. What's your pleasure?" Kelsie was holding the thin needle in a gloved hand.

Pam flexed her eyebrows. She really wanted to attack the wrinkle at the corner of her mouth, but knew her eyes should be smoothed out. Besides, she didn't know when Kelsie would be able to swipe another syringe full of the wonder drug. She adjusted in the folding chair and grabbed the mirror on the small table next to her.

Mirrors don't lie, although Pam wished they

did.

Each time she looked at herself, she'd crumble a little more. Age, the killer of all things beauty, was catching her and catching her fast. She wished Kelsie had another 200 units with her, but that was out of the question. It wouldn't have mattered anyway; Pam couldn't afford it. This one session was going to set her back and she might have to skimp on her next shipment of products. As much as she hated the cunt, Denise's jar of cream was a great replacement and would save her money.

Pam examined her face, knowing she had to make a decision and soon. She put the mirror down.

"Made up your mind?" Kelsie asked, the syringe still in her hand.

"Do the eyes," Pam said, leaning her head back. "They're the window to the soul."

Kelsie put her free hand on Pam's face, finding her mark for the needle to enter. "Yeah, but you have to have one first," she joked, pressing gently on the plunger.

The joke, one made a million times over, struck Pam like something physical.

Do I have a soul? Does anyone? Or is my God trapped in the mirror, hiding behind smooth flesh and toned muscle? Her thoughts raced as Kelsie shifted to the other eye.

"And...done," Kelsie capped the needle and set it on the table.

Pam's mind snapped out of her theological debate with itself and back to the present. She sat up, feeling the chemical in her flesh, working its magic, restoring her youth. Quickly, she dug through her purse and pulled out an ice mask.

Kelsie smiled and snapped her gloves off. "You know you can do that at home?" She watched as Pam adjusted the blue-gel filled masked over her eyes and forehead.

"Yes, but I *cannot* have any bruising this time." The first time she'd gotten an injection, it looked like she went 10 rounds with a boxer. She burned a good chunk of sick time as not to be seen.

Kelsie laughed and said, "Relax, I'm much better now."

It was true, that was for sure, but still, Pam wasn't risking it. Especially with Denise flaunting her tits around the office.

"Yeah, well I'm not taking the risk."

It had been almost six months since their agreement had been made and like any relationship, there were ups and downs.

Kelsie worked for a well-known plastic surgeon in the downtown section of the city. Her doctor wasn't the best, but he was pretty affordable, when it came to plastic surgery.

Pam, knowing this, decided to make an appointment for a consultation. Dr. Mahmoud sat down with her, listening to her gripes about her body and saw the dollar signs rising. He assured Pam she could have the body of a 22-year-old again, and the breasts of a teenager. During the meeting, Pam lit up, thinking about erasing the damages of time, until it came to the financial part.

Her company had pretty good health insurance and she definitely had a sickness: old age. But, when she tried to submit the claim for thousands of dollars of plastic surgery, her insurance company promptly told her to 'fuck off' in a very professional way.

That was where Nurse Kelsie came in. With a quick look in Pam's file for a phone number and a few sticky fingers, Kelsie and Pam were able to set up a little agreement.

Pam adjusted the ice mask, feeling the cold reducing the swelling. She had a question for Kelsie, one she'd asked before and would ask again.

"Have you given any thought to what I asked you last time?"

Kelsie was playing on her phone, smiling at something stupid. She stopped and looked at the masked woman sitting in the chair.

"I told you, this shit is risky enough. There's no way I can do more. End. Of. Story." Kelsie spat the last word.

Pam adjusted, leaning closer. "Come on, you can't sneak me in at night? I'm sure you could give me a little lipo; you're good at your job."

Kelsie gave her a look. "Yes, I am, and I'd like to keep that job, thank you very much." This conversation was like a broken record. Every time,

Pam was looking for more. The Botox was great, but it wore off. The more damage to the skin and muscle, the quicker the effects faded. She was never satisfied. After hearing about Denise's new implants, Kelsie knew she was going to be questioned again.

"Is there anyone else who might do things," Pam searched for the right words as not to offend her only connection in the plastic surgery world, "under the table?"

Kelsie stood, signaling it was time to go. Any other time she would've laughed at Pam in the stupid ice mask, but she didn't. There was something cold in her eyes and it wasn't the frozen gel.

"Listen," Kelsie paused, not wanting to cross this bridge, but knowing it was the only way out of it. She was sick of dealing with Pam's questions, but the money from the swiped Botox was good. If she gave her a lead, albeit a weak one, maybe she'd leave her the fuck alone. "There's a doctor I've heard of, okay. He hasn't practiced in a while, but there's rumors around the office he's back in town. Now, I can't vouch for his skills, but before he stopped practicing, he was supposedly one of the best."

Pam smiled. "Great, who is he? Why did he stop? Is he expensive?" She had a million more questions, but Kelsie stopped her with a raised hand.

"I don't know much, but I'll text you what I

do know, if that will get you to stop begging me."

"Yes, yes, of course." Pam was beaming. "I'm sorry, you just do great work and I want to be pretty."

Kelsie cringed. Her nose wrinkled like she'd smelled something foul. She regained her composure, just slightly.

"Okay, I'm sending you what I've heard. This may not be legit, but it's the best I can do." Her finger hovered over the screen. "But you'll no longer ask me to do anything else, understand?"

Pam was nodding furiously. "I won't even make a peep the next time I'm here. Scout's honor," she said, holding up her hand. Her smile was wide, and with the ice mask over her eyes, she looked like a deranged super hero.

Kelsie, against her better judgement, hit send.

Pam's phone dinged at the new text message. She glanced at the info, making sure it was real.

"If he was so good, why hasn't he practiced in so long?" Pam asked, standing up and putting on her jacket.

Kelsie laughed. "It's kind of hard to do boob jobs in prison." She pressed the button for the garage door opener. "See yourself out."

Chapter 3

Pam woke up feeling like shit.

After her backdoor-Botox with Kelsie, she went straight home. Her ice mask was starting to warm up and she didn't want to swell or bruise. The swelling was an issue, but more than that was the thought of this doctor. This disgraced doctor... who could help her.

When she'd finally made it home, Pam's mind was racing with possibilities. Could this doctor make her pretty? As beautiful as she *deserved* to be or would he be another quack, looking to get laid or rip her off? No, she trusted Kelsie when it came to plastic surgery. But still, it would be pricey. Even if she was able to find this guy and convince him to help her, she'd still have to pay. That could be a problem. Well, maybe he was the type looking for some pussy. She'd give a blowjob or lay on her back for a few minutes if that meant a little liposuction or even better, a boob job. The guy was in prison and if he was older, he probably didn't see much action when he was released. Pam was pretty sure they could work something out.

These thoughts and more ran her mind ragged as the minutes and hours on the clock continued to tick by. Finally, after the pain of exhaustion was too much, she fell asleep, only to be woken by a shrill alarm clock.

Pam had snoozed her alarm once, which meant part of her routine would be sacrificed. When the alarm blared again, she smacked the snooze for a second time, knowing that would be the last. The third alarm finally pulled her from bed, but she knew she'd pay for it.

The Botox went well and she wasn't swollen, or God forbid, bruised. Her forehead had two little red dots, which were easily concealed with coverup. But, her eyes. Her eyes weren't swollen or bruised, but it was quite evident she hadn't slept well.

Pam rushed around her apartment, getting ready. She was so behind she didn't even have time for any self-loathing in front of the mirror. She packed her unsatisfactory breasts away in a padded bra and started in on her face.

"Fuck," she said to her reflection, as she leaned close to the makeup mirror in the bathroom. She didn't think her cream would do much to lessen the tired look. Maybe she'd go with a bolder shade of eye makeup, hopefully drawing from the fact she looked like shit. Then, she remembered the expensive cream Denise had given her.

Pam ran out of the bathroom like she was on fire and grabbed her purse. The day prior, when that cunt, Denise, had given her the jar, she considered throwing it away. Even she wasn't crazy enough to do that, as much as she couldn't stand the little twat. Pam took it from her purse and went back into the bathroom. She applied the magical cream to her face, and checked the time.

"Fuck," she was going to miss her bus if she didn't hustle. Pam fanned her face, willing the cream to dry faster, and quickly applied her makeup. With only minutes to spare, she left her apartment and headed to the office.

Pam's head drooped as her fingers hovered over the keyboard. She shook herself awake and reached for her coffee. The bitter drink made her cringe, but she needed the caffeine to get through the day. She also knew she would be applying a heavy dose of teeth whitener that night to counteract the staining of the beverage. Pam put the Styrofoam cup down, adjusted her chair and grabbed another sheet to enter.

The day was mundane at best. Denise and her new tits were still talked about, but she'd come to work dressed a little more conservative. Her chest was still on full display, but when you had a boob job that cost as much as a luxury car, you didn't pack them away.

Pam's trained fingers lurched over the keyboard, each manicured nail striking a key. She'd finished and looked up, peeking over her cubicle wall. She wished she hadn't.

Denise was walking towards her and their eyes met. It was only a moment, but it was there.

Pam snapped her head down, grabbing another form. She knew she looked like shit and felt even worse, and the last thing she wanted to do was deal with Denise. She snatched another paper from her stack and began typing. The smell of *Joy Baccarat* flooded her nostrils.

Get the fuck away from me, you fucking cunt! Pam's fingers itched to grab the letter opener and plunge it into Denise's face. Just her presence, her smell, her aura, it made Pam seethe. Each day Pam aged, becoming more and more human, while Denise, little miss perfect, seemed to defy time. A goddess amongst farm animals.

You fucking cow!

Denise stood next to Pam's cubicle, waiting to be acknowledged. She wouldn't wait long.

Pam did what she could to ignore the woman, focusing on her task at hand, but it was quite obvious she was standing there, torturing her. She hit the last keystroke a little harder than necessary and turned.

"Oh, hey, Denise." Pam did her best to act startled, but it sounded canned and fake, even to her. "What's up?" she asked, grabbing another sheet from the bin.

Denise stood there. The air of perfection seemed to flow from her like noxious fumes. She'd forgone the slutty dress for the day, opting for a white blouse and black skirt. It was simple, but she made it look like it belonged on a runway in Paris or Milan. Her buttons were undone just enough to not show too much cleavage, but only a peek at those perfect breasts. The material was high quality, of course, but just sheer enough to show the outline of her lace bra.

Pam looked at the other woman, her eyes drinking in the perfection of her body. Anger and jealousy gave her an unwelcomed adrenaline dump. She tried not to stare, but was nearly eye-level with Denise's chest, so that was a losing battle.

Perfect, smooth, full, taut, perky, desired. Bitch, whore, cunt. I fucking hate you! Images flashed in Pam's mind: her now coffee-stained teeth ripping Denise's nose off, carving her name in her flat, toned midsection. The pain in those adorable eyes...

Denise looked down on her and flashed a perfect smile.

Pam smiled, but did her best to not show too much of her teeth. She knew she would be finishing her coffee and have to brush after her hellish confrontation.

"Oh, not much. I just wrapped up my

workload for the morning and figured I'd stop by to say hi." She looked at Pam's bin, her workload, which seemed to be growing on its own.

Pam knew what she was looking at, but didn't dare move her head. She just kept her plastic smile on her face, looking at the youthful beauty in front of her.

How would you like it if I knocked those pretty fucking teeth from your mouth? Would Bradley still want to fuck as much, or would he not care if his whore wife fucked around? Oh no, he would buy you new teeth, better teeth, teeth that would retract when you are sucking his cock. But what if I cut out your tongue? Pretty hard to give a decent blowjob without that. But you'd find a fucking way. Women like you always find a fucking way.

Pam's smile was hurting her face. The sudden thought of seeing Denise on the ground, spitting the shattered remains of her pearly whites, was enough to bring her a little glimmer of joy. She could almost feel the severed tongue in her grasp. Like a giant gummy worm, rough and warm, dripping gore.

Denise turned her attention from Pam's workload and back to the woman. She looked at her, and furrowed her brows.

Pam's smile abated, and a feeling of panic, one she'd felt the day before, had returned.

"Oh, Pammy," Denise said, almost shrieking. "Are you feeling alright? Getting enough sleep?" She leaned over, giving Pam a full view down her shirt.

Pam, for all of her panic, did glance down Denise's blouse. Her suspicions were confirmed; Denise's boob job was damn near perfection.

"I—I feel fine, why?" Pam muttered, wanting to touch her face. To hide her hideous face from the prying eyes of Denise. The Botox looked good, she knew that, but maybe she'd rushed her makeup a little too much. Did she fuck it up? Smear it maybe? In her dozing, did she smudge her eyeliner, making her look like she'd been punched in the face? Or even worse, forget to blend it at her neck? There was nothing more ridiculous than a woman that looked like she was wearing a mask of foundation.

Panic!

Denise let out a little moan, the one usually reserved for a child. For a child that shows you a finger painting made of their own shit.

"You look," Denise said, standing back up straight, "tired. That's all." She smiled, watching Pam crumble. "It could be nothing, but make sure you're using the cream I gave you. I know it's a bit pricy, but what's a few dollars compared to a life of beauty." Her smile was still there as she leaned back in. "It has some anti-aging elements in it, to help tighten up and get rid of those wrinkles."

Pam was on the verge of tears and murder. The hot sting of them burned her nostrils, making her want to sneeze. To blow a fucking wad of snot on the face of perfection. *Maybe I'll use a knife to carve some wrinkles in your perfect skin. Flay you open, slice that bright smile away. Cut your fucking eyelids off, so you can always see what an ugly bitch you are. How fucking vile I made you. Bitch!*

"Ok, Pammy, I'll see you for lunch," Denise said, turning to walk away. The cloud of perfume followed her, and with it Pam's soul.

Pam kicked her apartment door shut, rattling the walls. She threw her purse on the counter and fell onto the couch. Then, the tears came.

After her encounter with Denise, Pam held it together. She focused on her work and pecked away, willing her battered mind to think of anything else. It was for naught.

You look tired. That's all. Kept playing over and over in her head. On repeat. All fucking day. That smile. That perfect smile. That perfect face. That perfect body. That perfect fucking life. Over and over, *You look tired. That's all.* It rattled in her brain, bouncing around. Each strike caused damage, digging deep into her psyche. Until finally, something broke. Pam felt it when it happened. She felt herself snap, like a cable under tension finally giving way. Flailing wildly, taking limbs and destroying all in her wake.

The day in the locker room, twenty years

earlier. That's what it was like. The shame and embarrassment when that curtain flew open, showing her nudity. This was the same, but Denise didn't yank a physical curtain, but pulled the one from her, revealing her inner ugliness. The monster inside of her was exposed to the light.

Pam felt hot and cold, like the day in the snow. The day her fucking mother found her, stopping her. The next day she was taken to the hospital, the fucking *psych ward,* even though they don't call it that anymore. She emerged days later, like she'd been reborn. Given ways to cope, to make herself feel good. It was all bullshit. She knew what would make her feel better: bloodshed. It was wrong, so fucking wrong, but it beckoned to her, calling like a siren in the sea, willing her to drown herself in gore, in the saltiness of her enemies. She wouldn't act on it, as much as it willed and begged. But oh fuck, did she want to.

And then in the spring, she'd finally gotten Ashley, making the queen of *the cunts* a monster. It was deemed an accident, but they knew, they all fucking knew. Above all, Ashley knew and from that day on, after the surgeries of course, she didn't even fucking look at Pam. Not a side glance, not a word of remorse...nothing. She just kept her face down, hidden in the crowds and pointing fingers. The day Pam saw the once beautiful girl crying after a few boys laughed at her was one of the best days in her life. *She* did that. Pam made that monster, but she'd made a second one too:

herself.

But this was different. A different time in her life, yet still, that high school girl begged to come out. That girl that saw her classmate mangled and bloodied. She knew that at that moment, if Denise was in front of her, she wouldn't have been able to control herself. She would've beat her bloody. Stomped her face, ripped out her hair. Popped her implants. It would've been a sin to destroy something so beautiful, but she would've relished in it.

Pam ugly-cried into a decorative pillow on the couch. She screamed into it, the hot tears flowing as if a dam had broken open. The battle in her raged, hot and fierce, and she was losing. But was she? The cracks deepened, letting the blackness leak out.

In the back of her mind she heard her phone ding with a notification. It was probably a stupid email, but it snapped her out of her misery. Something else came back to her: the doctor, the disgraced plastic surgeon.

After she'd gotten back from Kelsie's, her brain wouldn't stop thinking about this mystery man and how he could help her. That morning, he'd all but been forgotten, until then.

Pam grabbed her phone and looked at the info Kelsie had given her. She walked into the bathroom and turned on the bright lights. Any other time she would've been horrified by the reflection staring back at her: snotty nose, running makeup, red eyes, but not at that moment. At that moment she looked fierce and pretty.

She was pretty, but Dr. Joseph DiBiro would make her beautiful.

Chapter 4

The next day Pam woke with a sense of purpose and desire. She had a plan, albeit not a great one. But first, she needed to call in sick from work. It wasn't even a call-in anymore; it was an email. She simply sent Mr. Rosamilia a quick email with a leave request attached and *boom* she was out sick.

Pam laid in bed with her cellphone. She hadn't even been to the bathroom yet, but if she was going to seek out Dr. DiBiro, she wanted to do a little research on him first. His name popped up immediately.

"*Dr. Dirty*, now that's not very promising," Pam said aloud as she read the article.

Dr. Joseph DiBiro was arrested today on charges of medical malpractice. After a six-month investigation by the state Attorney General's Office, Dr. DiBiro was finally relieved of duty. The full details have yet to be made available, but sources indicate Dr. DiBiro has been accused of sexually and physically assaulting patients, who were under anesthesia. One woman, who spoke with our reporters, stated she had a routine tummy tuck surgery. A common procedure for a skilled plastic surgeon. When healed, she continued to feel pain behind the incision site. The pain intensified, bringing our source to seek further medical attention. What was discovered will chill you to the core. Click the link to read more.

Pam didn't feel like reading more; she didn't care. She scrolled on, finding a few more articles, only reading snippets.

...sore nipples after a rhinoplasty...

...faint carving of initials in flesh with a scalpel...

...gangrenous infections caused by unknown fluid in incision site. Possible semen...

...uncontrollable rectal leakage and bleeding...

Pam stopped all together after the bloody, leaky asshole. She put her phone down and draped her forearm over her face.

What the fuck am I thinking? she asked herself. *Do I want a quack, a pervert cutting into me?* She laid there with her mind racing, thinking of the pros and cons of even trying to seek Joe DiBiro out. Again, she picked up her cellphone, this time activating the camera.

The lens was pointed at the ceiling and nervously, she switched it to the front facing camera. She looked like microwaved dog shit. Her hair was a mess and a few strands of gray were peeking out. Her face was even worse. The injection sites from the Botox were healing nicely, but a subtle and almost non-existent bruising was starting to show. Her eyes were dark and decorated with bags and broken blood vessels. Even her mouth was looking bad, with the creasing by her lips only getting worse.

Yes, she could use the mad doctor, *Dr. Dirty*, as the article so plainly put. At that moment, she would do anything to be beautiful and Dr. DiBiro was going to help her.

Joe pushed a large broom down the aisle of the hardware store. There wasn't much to clean up, only some sawdust and a few stray screws, but it kept him busy. It wasn't his first choice of work, but the state parole office said he needed gainful employment and since he wasn't even allowed to look at a scalpel, this was it. Joe fucking hated it, but who could blame him. After years of school, training and being one of the top surgeons on the east coast, he was reduced to janitorial work for damn near minimum wage. That was no way for a man in his sixties to spend his life.

No, his life should've been full of hard days of work, making people better versions of themselves, late night dinners with his wife and God willing, bouncing a grandchild on his knee. But his life was far from that.

Instead, it was half-frozen dinners in front

of an antique TV, nightmares of prison and the torture he faced there, feeling dehumanized at having to piss in a cup in front of his dyke of a parole officer. And family? The day he was convicted was the last day he'd seen any of them. Gone, like dandelion fluff on the wind.

This was his life now, pushing the broom with an aching back and swollen feet. Emptying garbage cans, hoping they weren't too heavy. Avoiding his prick of an assistant manager, who would constantly ride him over the smallest, fucking thing. Joe didn't belong there. He belonged in the operating room, making art out of flesh and plastic. His mind wandered back to the glory days. The days of turning blobs of skin and fat into a pair of tits that would make people weep. The sound of cracking a nose, only to fix it and make it better. And then, there were his other *vices*. The feel of his gloved fingers in an unknowing vagina, while he jerked himself off through his gown. The sliminess of his semen, sitting like a cold oyster in his briefs. Each move reminding him of his patient's warmth. The feeling of carving his initials into the scar tissue of a tummy tuck, after all of the dawdling nurses left and he stayed to ensure the patient was resting easy. The touch of his blade, forbidden at the moment, cutting through swollen meat. Any good artist signs their work, so why shouldn't he? It was the best of times for him, a time when he was a god. A time long gone

Joe pushed the broom, the hypnotic sound

of it *swooshing* over the concrete floor lulled him, giving him a small reprieve. The loud speaker ripped him from the relaxation with a start.

"Clean-up on aisle six for a paint spill. Clean-up on aisle six for a paint spill."

"Fuck," Joe muttered, hoping no customers heard him. He checked his watch, one of the last relics of his former life, and realized Chris, the other janitor, had just started his break. Joe pushed his pile of dirt to one of the associate phones attached to a pillar and picked it up.

"Yeah, this is Joe," he said, after being connected to the last caller. "How much?" He looked up in disgust and anger. "Five fucking gallons?" Again, he looked around to make sure no one was in earshot. "Ok, yup, I'm on my way. Just close the aisle down and I'll handle it." He hung up without saying goodbye.

Joe picked up his broom, leaving his pile of debris abandoned, and headed towards the supply room. He never once noticed the woman in sunglasses, watching him.

Pam had left the house unshowered and not covered in make-up, a rarity for her to say the least. It felt uncomfortable, but she needed to blend in, and having a full face of fresh make-up was one way to get noticed. For once in her life, she wanted to blend in, not stand out.

The hardware store, a large chain-operated building, was an establishment she'd never set foot in. Luckily for her, it wasn't a far walk from a bus stop she was familiar with.

The store was big and loud and stunk of wood shavings. She didn't know what she was going to do yet, but she had to see Dr. DiBiro. She had to make sure he was real.

The sunglasses weren't the most original disguise, but they worked to not only conceal her identity, but to hide the hideousness of her eyes. Not that anyone would recognize her, but it was better to be safe than sorry.

Pam wandered around the store, touching things aimlessly as she looked for the disgraced doctor. She checked every register and counter, thinking a man with his education would be doing some kind of desk work. Not to mention, he was in his sixties, so hard labor probably wasn't in the cards.

She'd watched an old man with a push broom moving down the aisle, ushering a pile of dirt in front of him. He was clearly in some kind of discomfort, but that seemed to come with age. Age, something no one could escape. The man turned slightly, just enough for Pam to see his profile.

Her heart, which had since calmed from the excitement of coming to the store, began racing anew. It was him; she was sure of it. She'd spent the rest of the morning online looking him up. Not anymore of his criminal allegations, no, those she didn't give a fuck about. Pam had busied herself with looking up his surgeries. The women he'd brought out of the mundane and thrust into the spotlight. The happy testimonials and pictures from their procedures. Small breasts made full and large. Crooked noses straightened. Loose, stretch-marked stomachs turned into flat, works of art. This man was a genius; an artist with a scalpel, and Pam couldn't wait to be his next canvas.

She was lost in a daydream, a daydream of Denise crying, her face ugly and chest flat. Pam would come sauntering in, a beautiful pair of tits, thick ass, firm skin, and stop. She'd look at the weeping woman—so full of self-doubt and self-hatred—and laugh. She'd say, *'oh, you look tired,'* and grin, watching tears slide down her pimpled face.

The loudspeaker made her jump and she realized it had done the same to Dr. DiBiro. *What was his daydream about?* she wondered. The speaker blared about a clean-up for a paint spill. She saw him look at his watch in frustration and walk over to a phone. More frustration as he spoke and hung up. He grabbed his broom and walked away.

That was ok, Pam had time. She could wait. For beauty, she'd wait forever.

Chapter 5

Pam didn't know how long Dr. DiBiro would be, but she decided to wait him out. She wandered the few shops around the nearest bus stop, hoping he'd be using the public transportation. It was a guess, but she figured his salary, much like hers, wasn't enough for a car. Just before dark, her hunch paid off.

Joe DiBiro didn't look like much, but to Pam, he was a port in a storm. A storm of vanity, jealousy and beauty. She watched him walk towards the bus stop. He was in his sixties, but looked much older. His shoulders were slightly hunched and his eyes were downcast. He had a full head of gray hair, but it wasn't cut very well. It had the look of a homemade hack job.

Pam had been preparing for this moment the entire day, waiting and rehearsing what she'd say. Closer and closer he walked, until he was about to sit on the bench.

Joe sat down, letting out a weary sigh as he did. He put his hands to his lower back and stretched, releasing a few loud pops.

Pam's mouth was a desert. Her tongue clung to the roof of her mouth and she tried to work up enough spit to talk to him. Her speech, the one she'd prepared, flew from her mind. She grabbed at it, like it was something physical, trying to find the words. She was staring at him, but he was oblivious, just watching a piece of plastic dance in the light breeze.

Slowly, he turned his head towards her. Pam, even though she was still wearing the sunglasses, felt their eyes lock. It wasn't a sexual or even an attractive connection, but something different. Something almost primal. Like two kindred spirits finding each other in the dark. She opened her mouth to speak.

"Dr. Di—," she began.

"About fucking time," Joe said, standing as the bus rolled up and stopped with a hiss.

Pam felt the air rush out of her with the brakes. The courage seemed to pour from her body, but she wouldn't be defeated. No, Pamela Rose was no fucking quitter. She followed him onto the bus, deciding she'd get off with him. That would give her some more time to come up with a better speech, or try to remember the one she had earlier.

She didn't sit by him, as badly as she wanted to. Their conversation wasn't one for public transportation, that was for sure.

The bus rumbled through the fast-approaching darkness. Street lights began to drop pools of a buttery glow below them and stores were lit up.

Pam watched Joe, who was staring out of the window. His head bobbed with exhaustion and he rested it against the dirty glass. His breath left condensation as he drifted to sleep.

The bus began to slow down and pull over; another stop on its journey through the city. Pam hoped it was his stop; she knew the fare to get home was going to be pricey the further they went.

Joe jumped, his nap interrupted when the bus slowed to a halt. He looked around, confused and realized it was his stop.

Pam grabbed her purse and decided it was time to lose the sunglasses. They looked odd indoors during the day, but wearing them at night was no good. She didn't want to look crazy.

Joe stepped off the bus, with Pam right behind him. The sidewalk was empty as the pair began walking.

Pam's reserve was back and stronger than ever. She cleared her throat.

"Doctor DiBiro," she said, loud enough to get his attention, but not screaming it.

Joe didn't stop, but he did hesitate for just a moment.

That was more than enough to confirm his identity in Pam's eyes. She walked faster, almost within range to touch him.

"Doctor DiBiro." This time she put a little authority in her voice.

Joe stopped and shuddered.

Pam didn't know if he was mad, upset or a combination of both.

"Look," he said, not turning around. His voice quivered, but he spoke. "I don't want to give an interview, nor do I want to talk. I just want to get home, eat, and go to bed. Is that too much to ask?"

Pam hard swallowed, hearing the pain in his voice. The tiredness.

"No," she croaked, "it's not too much. But I need you." She licked her lips, which felt dry in the cool breeze.

Joe turned and saw the woman standing in front of him. He'd seen the likes of her thousands of times over. Mid to late 30s, putting on a little weight, tits starting to head south and face looking like the roadmap to get there. He made a fortune off of women like the one in front of him. Made art from their bodies, shaping fat, bone and plastic into masterpieces. Even though he hadn't touched a blade in years, he was sizing her up, thinking of what he'd do to her. What he'd do to make her beautiful.

"I'm not a reporter, I swear," Pam stepped closer. Close enough to smell his aftershave, Aqua Velva if she wasn't mistaken. "My name is Pam. A friend told me about you. She said you could help me."

Joe could feel his heart racing. His pulse was throbbing in his brain, but it was a feeling of life.

Of a past time. A past life, which was no more. Never again.

"I'm not sure what you've heard," he said, his Adam's apple bobbing as he swallowed. "But I can't help you." He looked down and stuffed his hands into his jacket pocket. "I'm not much use to anyone anymore."

Pam stepped closer still. She was inches from him now, almost face to face. She could see the sadness in his eyes. The sadness of wasted talent.

"Yes, you can." Tears, abrupt tears, stung Pam's eyes.

Joe looked up at her.

"I want to be beautiful," she said, at almost a whisper.

He could do it. He could make her beautiful. A nip here, a tuck there. A few shots of Botox, a fresh pair of breasts, maybe remove a little fat. It wouldn't take much. She could be perfect.

"Listen," he said, the stress and tiredness of a hard day's work catching up to him. "I'm not in the business anymore and frankly, I'm fucking exhausted." Almost on cue, he yawned, revealing a beautiful set of teeth, that were clearly veneers.

Sensing her opportunity was fading, Pam grabbed him by the shoulders.

"Please," she begged. "I need your help."

Joe had dealt with crazies before, but it had been some time. Then again, what was crazy? Was he crazy for things he did? Was he crazy for seeing no harm in a little experimentation or leaving his mark? Was he crazy for contemplating helping this woman? The excitement in her eyes, the desire for perfection…the begging. It all reignited something ancient, something that lay dormant in his soul. Something that would never die. He shuddered, knowing it was a bad idea; what he was about to do. Gently, he removed her hands from his shoulders.

"I'm off tomorrow and have some free time in my schedule." By free time he meant the entire day. "Give me your number and wait. I'll call you and we can talk. I still have some connections, albeit weak ones."

Pam took a deep breath. It wasn't perfect, but it was a start.

"Yes, yes of course. My number." She opened her purse, looking and praying she had a pen and something to write on. There was no pen, only her lip stain. She dug further, hoping for something to put her number down on. Panic was setting in. She could feel him getting anxious, to be done with this encounter and on his way. A gust of wind blew and with it came a few pieces of city trash. Pam grabbed a wayward burger wrapper and ripped off the cleanest piece. She wrote her number as clearly as possible.

"Here," she said, handing it to him.

Joe took the greasy wax paper and looked it over. "Okay," he replied, folding it and putting it in his jacket pocket. "I'll be in touch." He turned and without another word, walked away.

Pam was on cloud-nine, knowing her life was about to change. She walked back to the bus stop and sat on the bench, hoping the next bus would be by soon.

Joe closed his apartment door and leaned against it. His mind was a blur and he reached into his pocket and pulled out the wrapper. For a moment, he couldn't find it. He didn't think he'd lost it, but feared he'd imagined the entire thing. That the crazy woman who wanted plastic surgery was fake, and his urge to create had overwhelmed his abused psyche. When he unfolded the paper and saw the number, he knew he wasn't cracking up. Just crazy for even taking it.

Joe put the paper on his fridge, afraid if he put it on the table, it would get thrown away. Not that he was one for cleaning often, but it was a possibility.

He opened the freezer and grabbed a plastic bottle of vodka. He took a dirty cup, dumped out whatever was in it, and poured himself a drink. Within two gulps, he downed it and refilled the cup.

Joe went into his bedroom with his drink in hand. He set the cup on his nightstand and knelt down on the floor, looking under the bed. He slid out an old tote and opened it. Inside were a few photo albums, one of which he took out. With his drink back in hand, he went out to the living room.

The room was sparse with only a TV, recliner and coffee table, but it was all he needed.

Joe plopped into the chair, and set the album down. He polished off his second drink, which was larger than the first. The slight sensation of euphoria was kicking in and he decided he didn't want another. At least not yet.

He flipped open the album. It was his art. Some of his greatest work. Before, during and after pictures, most of which were clinically done. But some, were far from that.

Polaroids of him with his cock in incisions. Of him with his scalpel to an exposed eye. Even one of him sodomizing a sleeping man with a variety of instruments, making his anus look like it was sprouting a bouquet of metal.

These were his works of art. He flipped through, seeing what he'd done. The body art he'd created, along with satisfying his own perversions. He smiled and touched them, remembering, feeling the warmth of their flesh through the pages.

Joe slammed the book shut with a slap.

No, that was a former life. That was another man, in a different world. A sick man, or so the *doctors* said. That was a man who went to prison and had the sickness beaten and raped out of him.

No, he was just Joe the janitor now. Dr. DiBiro was dead and buried.

He got up, taking his glass with him. The vodka was sweating on the counter and he decided to go against his better judgement and have another drink. His eyes wandered, but they weren't lost; they knew exactly what they were looking for.

The phone number on the refrigerator stared back at him. He knew Dr. DiBiro wasn't dead yet. And he had art to create.

Chapter 6

Pam slept like shit. The entire night her mind raced, coming up with scenarios and images of what she *could* look like.

She took another sick day, but was starting to think it was a mistake. It was nearing 2 pm and Dr. DiBiro hadn't called. She constantly checked her phone, making sure it was on and had service, but it refused to ring

That was her day; staring at her phone. She didn't even shower for fear of missing his call. One day of not showering was okay, but now she was into her second, which for her was a rarity.

Pam put a manicured nail into her mouth and gave it a little nibble. It was a vice she'd had since childhood, a nervous tick, which decided to show its ugly head again. The heavily lacquered nail cracked and a thin layer came off into her mouth.

"Fuck," she said, looking at her handy work. She hadn't meant to take so much, just a little bit. Now, she'd ruined the whole nail. Jagged white shone where the paint used to be. $30 wasted. Well, since that finger was ruined, she'd might as well chomp it down.

She chewed, switching from one finger to the next. It didn't matter, one phone call could change her life. Could set her free. Could allow the butterfly in her to be unleashed on the world.

Another nail was spat onto the floor as the phone began to ring. At first, Pam thought she was hearing things. That her mind was playing tricks on her. She snapped out of it, and grabbed the phone from the table.

"Hello," she said before the call even completely connected.

There was silence for a second and she thought maybe it was a telemarketer and then a voice spoke.

"Hello, Pam?"

It was him, holy fuck it was him. Pam could've levitated with joy and anticipation. She thrust another finger into her mouth, pulling the nail off quickly. The cuticle was exposed and bleeding, but she didn't mind. The stinging felt good, like she was alive.

"Yes, yes, it's me," she said, grinning. She tucked her legs underneath her on the couch.

"Listen, I'm not sure what I can do for you," Joe said, with slow speech. "But we can meet up and talk, if that's okay?"

"Of course, yes. That's perfectly fine. When and where?" In that moment, anyone seeing Pam's face would've thought she'd won the lottery. Her hair was a mess, skin greasy with a few blossoming pimples and eyes dark, but boy oh boy was she happy.

"Can you do four at Latham Park?"

Latham Park wasn't too far for her. Only a short bus ride at best. Either way, she'd be there even if she had to carjack someone.

"Yes, I'll be there." She could taste the sourness of her breath and wasn't sure if she'd even brushed her teeth. "I just have to get cleaned up and I'll meet you there."

Joe didn't answer. Pam checked her phone to make sure she hadn't dropped the call. The line was still active and she put it back to her ear. She opened her mouth to speak.

"I'll see you there," he said quickly and hung up.

Pam looked at the phone like it was a dream. Finally, a consultation with a real doctor, and one of the best. She couldn't believe her luck. But first, she desperately needed a shower.

Pam walked into the bathroom and turned on the water. Steam rose from behind the curtains, filling the room. She stripped naked and stared at her hazy reflection. It was like a dream, like looking at a body she shouldn't have. Even in the obstruction of the mist, she could see her flaws. The darkness of her eyes, the oily skin, the new pimples, and her biggest nemesis, her breasts.

Pam cupped her chest again, but this time

she didn't feel pity or sadness, but anger. She pinched her nipples, squeezing them between forefinger and thumb. She pulled, squeezing, as if wanting to rip them from her chest. The pain was electric, but almost euphoric, sexual. She let go and looked at her angry buds of pink flesh. Pam realized her pussy was wet, a hotness she hadn't felt in a long time.

She wiped the mirror free from steam and stared...and grinned. Her fingers explored the slickness of her cleft, rolling her clit, pushing it hard.

The steam continued to pour from the shower, which was more like a sauna. Pam opened the curtain, entered, and detached the shower head. Gently, she lowered herself to the shower floor and placed the burning hot nozzle between her legs. The pleasure and pain were overwhelming, but the heat was what she needed. The fiery water scalded her, but it also cleansed. Her fingers replaced the water jet, as she bathed her chest in the heat. She wanted to burn them, to roast her breasts from her body. To melt them away and let them grow anew. Pam's hand was a blur, rubbing herself and burning her battered breasts at the same time. The pain of the water was almost too much, but it was just what she needed to climax. Finally, after her tormented breasts couldn't handle it anymore, she came. Shudders of pain and pleasure made her quiver. The aftershock of the orgasm had her vision swimming, like she'd been struck in the head.

Pam felt like she was bathed in fire. Like her old self had been burned away. Like she was a phoenix. And like a phoenix, she'd rise from the ashes, born anew…and beautiful.

Joe looked at the phone. His hand was shaking, not quite believing that he'd actually called her. Her, a crazy woman who accosted him on the sidewalk. A woman who was clearly unstable. Yes, he'd called her and yes, he intended to meet with her. Maybe he was just as crazy as she was. Kindred spirits wrapped in the depths of shallowness and vanity.

For him, it was the satisfaction of creation. Creating something beautiful. Something fresh. Breathing new life into old skin. Rejuvenating love lives or starting new ones. And of course, it allowed him his own perversions. To experiment with flesh. To stare into the void of death, knowing one move or mistake could snuff out a life. The feeling of power over the unconscious patient. That they trust him with not only their looks, but their lives.

Fucking morons.

Joe set his phone down and picked up another photo album. He thumbed through it, passing all of the clinical pictures. He was searching for Polaroid's.

His fingers, which were so deft and nimble, touched one. It was one of his favorites.

It was a picture he'd taken of himself, years before 'selfies' were a thing. He was smiling, with his surgical mask pulled down and something in his teeth. He knew what it was, but the casual observer wouldn't.

That had been a good day for him. It was a breast reduction, something that was less common, but still a normal procedure. The patient, obviously, was well-endowed. Well, her back thought she was too *well*-endowed. The surgery had been a success, but Joe kept a little morsel out of the hazmat bag. It was a piece of her nipple. Not a very large one, but enough. He wanted to feel it in his mouth, to bite it...hard. He'd had plenty of nipples in his mouth before, some from women who were awake, others from those under anesthesia. But he never truly bit one. It was an itch he needed to scratch. He bit the nipple, chewed it up, but wouldn't swallow. He wasn't that fucking sick.

Joe flipped the page, reliving some of his greatest moments. He wondered if his greatest was yet to come.

Chapter 7

Pam sat on the park bench. The day was cool and getting colder, but with the sunshine, it was bearable. She wore a pair of jeans and an old hoodie. Her hair was pulled back into a pony tail and still damp from the shower. She hadn't worn a bra; her breasts were still tender from the abuse she'd inflicted on them earlier. Luckily, the sweatshirt was baggy enough to conceal that fact. She had her sunglasses, but didn't put them on. She wanted to be noticed by Dr. DiBiro and this time, had no need to hide.

She saw him approaching and did everything she could not to stand up and wave.

They locked eyes and she took a deep breath as he sat next to her.

"Nice to see you again," he said, giving her a nod. He looked away from her, staring straight ahead. "I'm not sure what you'd like from me."

Pam was looking at him, staring at the side of his face. She pulled her sunglasses out and put them on.

The park was almost empty in the middle of the day on a Wednesday, so she didn't mind speaking frankly.

"I want you to work on me. To make me beautiful."

Joe sighed and turned to face her. He wanted the same thing, but how that would be accomplished, he didn't know. He had the skills and knowhow, but it was the tools, and material he lacked. His old surgical bag, a gift from his parents decades ago, was still around and stocked. That didn't matter. He needed much more than tools for a procedure.

"I'm not sure I can help you," he said, watching her deflate slightly.

"Why not?" Her voice quivered. "I heard you were one of the best ever. A master, who could do almost anything."

Joe smiled at the flattery. It was true, he was fucking good. Being good couldn't make anesthesia appear, or Botox, or implants. They needed licensing and were monitored. He could probably scrounge up some knockoff material, but even that would be tricky.

"Yes, you've heard correctly, but a painter can't paint without paint. I need materials. I have nothing, besides some old tools. I'm sure I could chisel out some cartilage from your nose, but," he gave her an examining glance, "yours looks pretty damn good. Now, unless you have access to medical grade materials, there's not much I can do besides talk with you."

Pam stared at him in disbelief. She, for some reason, thought this would go differently. That he would have access to everything, using his old contacts. Not only that, but she thought maybe it would be cheap, since there was no insurance or expensive operating rooms. Suddenly, she felt fucking stupid.

"I'm sorry for dragging you out. I — I just wanted some help." She could feel herself breaking down.

"I'm sorry too, if you had a false sense of hope. If I could get my hands on some stuff, we'd be good. I could do whatever you wanted." A thought occurred to him. He had no idea what kind of surgery she was even looking for. She just wanted to be beautiful, which was too vague for him to go on. "By the way, what were you looking to do? I could ask around to see what's available, but it wouldn't be cheap."

Pam removed her sunglasses and wiped her eyes. The dark rings around them were quite obvious without makeup. She put the sunglasses back on and said, "Breast implants." Her mind wandered back to the abuse she'd inflicted on herself. She moved just a little, feeling her raw nipples rub the fabric of her shirt.

Joe gave a little smile, but it wasn't condescending. It was more of a *sorry, but that's pretty much impossible* smile.

"I wish I could help you, but quality breast

implants are nearly impossible to get without FDA approval and licensing. Something I can no longer obtain. Unless you have a pair lying around, that's out of the question."

In the back of her mind Pam knew it was going to come to this. This moment in her life when she'd cross a line. It was a question she'd asked herself over and over.

How far am I willing to go?

As far as I fucking can. There's no limit on beauty.

She now knew the answer to that question, but this equation needed more than just her. Pam paused, swallowed hard and took her glasses off again. This wasn't a conversation that should be obstructed by tinted glass. Her eyes, still dark around the edges, seemed clearer, with a sense of hope. She felt like the kid asking her parents for a sleepover, just praying they'd say yes.

"I can get them," she said, soft at first.

Joe's smile faded, his face going flat. "Say again?"

Pam licked her lips, which promptly curled into a grin, the same grin she'd seen in the mirror as she was plucking at her nipples. "I can get them. The tits, the implants. High quality. The best money can buy. I can get them to you."

Joe was stumped. "And how is that possible?"

Pam's grin widened, but faltered, quivering on the edges. "Can you take them out of someone?"

Denise won't mind. Good old Bradley will buy her a new pair, she thought.

"Out of a person and into you? Is that what you're asking me?" Joe asked, the disbelief thick in his voice. He'd done some pretty fucked up things in his career, but this was new to him. New... and challenging. A part of him felt the rush of excitement in his bowels. It was insane, highly illegal and immoral, but the part of him he'd recently unearthed was curious.

Pam nodded. "I have this bimbo at work. She's loaded and fully equipped with a brand-new pair of tits. The best around, or so she says." Pam looked away from him, her mind racing. "We can knock her out and cut them from her. Yeah, then you can put them in me." She looked back at him, that plastic smile splitting her face.

Joe stared, still thinking it was a joke. It was not, and seeing her face solidified that for him. He stood.

"Where are you going?" Pam asked, rising with him. "We need to discuss this. To plan it out." Panic dripped from her words.

Joe zippered his jacket. "You're sick," he said, turning to walk away. "You need help and I can't give that to you."

Pam stared. She wanted to chase him down. To tackle him to the ground. To smash his old face with her fists. She needed help? He stuck his cock in sleeping patients. He carved his fucking initials in scar tissue. He was a fucking monster, not her.

Her sanity was wavering, each second brought it closer to snapping.

"Fuck you!" she screamed, spit flying from her lips. "Fuck you, you fucking hack!" For a second, Joe slowed down, but only for a second. Pam put her sunglasses back on, hiding the windows to her soul, and stalked away.

Part 2 : ...Pain

May 1st 2002

Pam clenched the softball bat in her hands. She stepped out of the batter's box and took a few practice swings, hoping to get her timing right.

"Alright, Pam, give it a ride," Coach Braun yelled from behind the catcher. "Just keep your eye on the ball and watch the bat make contact."

Pam adjusted her helmet before stepping back into the box. *Mr. Braun, you should keep your eyes off the girls and more on the game, you sick fuck.* She thought. *I wonder what this bat would do to your fucking skull?*

"Yeah, fat chance, Coach Braun," Ashley said from the pitcher's mound. "This cow—I mean Pam—can't hit shit." The rest of the girls, most of the team was made up of *the cunts*, laughed.

Pam even heard a quick snicker from the coach, who did his best to stifle it. She knew he wanted to fuck Ashley—who didn't?—but had to maintain some kind of integrity.

"Okay, that's not necessary. We need this practice before Saturday's game, so focus, ladies."

He was back to his coach voice, but Pam knew. Oh, she fucking knew.

Pam stepped back into the box and clenched the bat. She looked out at Ashley, the queen of *the cunts* and focused.

Ashley held her glove up to her face, her beautiful face, and shook her head at the signs given by the catcher. Finally, she nodded and began her windup.

Pam watched, stared, ready to beat the piss out of the neon yellow ball.

Ashley's release was perfect, but Pam was fast with the bat. Pam had the ball lined up, watching it sail through the air. She started her swing…and missed.

The loud *pop* of the ball hitting the catcher's glove echoed.

Ashley looked smug, as she put her glove up for the catcher to throw the ball back.

"You have to be better than that, Bessie," Ashley said, smiling. Snickers came from the other players, not bothering to hide behind their gloves.

Even dirty and sweaty, Ashley was still beautiful. Just the right amount of color on her cheeks from the sun, the tasteful highlights she'd added to her hair, and even the little smear of dirt on her cheek.

Pam fucking hated her. Hated her more than anything. That fucking face. That beautiful, fucking face. Again, she squeezed the bat, but this time it wasn't aluminum…it was flesh. It was the thin neck of *the cunt* standing only forty-three feet from her. It was the soft feeling of her warm flesh succumbing to her grip, crushing the life from her. It was her tongue lolling out like that of a dead dog, left mangled on the side of the road. It was that fucking face.

Ashley adjusted her visor, cleared a little dirt from the rubber and settled in for the next pitch.

Pam heard Coach Braun behind her, but she didn't really *hear* him. He was talking, but her mind was gone. It was in another plane of existence. A place where the Ashley's of the world were as ugly in the flesh as they were in their attitudes. Her hands flexed again, squeezing more life from the bat, and she focused. She focused on the angelic bitch in front of her.

Ashley had her sign and pitched.

Pam didn't look at the ball, instead focusing on Ashley's face and only her face. The bat moved with almost superhuman speed, crushing the center of the ball. Pam felt the vibration through her arms, but the world seemed to slow down. For that, she was grateful. She could watch the entire thing and savor it.

The ball came back at Ashley and it came back hard. The wave of reality on her face was priceless. First, she knew she'd thrown a great pitch, one she thought was unhittable. Second, was the realization the bat made contact with the ball. Third, was fear, primal fear, as the large ball came flying right back at her face, knowing she'd never get her glove up in time.

The sound of Ashley's face breaking was almost as loud as the sound of the hit on the ball.

Bone shattered—not just broke, but shattered. The softball hit her on the tip of her chin, cracking it in half and taking most of her bottom teeth with it. Once that bone was obliterated, it continued its path to her cute little nose. Cartilage flexed and tore, leaving a distorted lump of broken and bloody meat in the center of Ashley's face. As the *coup de grâce*, the ball hit her left cheekbone with just enough force to break it, splitting the skin in the process.

Ashley went down in a heap, her hands going to her destroyed face.

"Holy shit!" Coach Braun yelled, running from behind the plate to check on his star pitcher.

The rest of the team came sprinting in as the girl created a cloud of dust from her pained writhing and screaming.

Pam stood at home with the bat still in her hand and smiled. She watched as Coach Braun nearly vomited when he saw the girl's mangled face. The other girls backed away, many of them crying and looking ill themselves.

Pam dragged the bat behind her, leaving a trail in the dirt as she approached the throng of players. She looked into the group, trying her hardest to see the injured girl. The sounds coming from the ground were heavenly. And then, she saw.

Pam gasped, but not in revulsion, but in awe. The blood caked with dirt, the white bone, the empty and broken tooth sockets.

The pain.

It was all beautiful. It felt like justice. Now, Ashley looked the way she acted: like a monster. And she did it. Pam did it, her. Little ole Pamela Rose had made a beauty queen into a beast. It was something she'd never thought possible. It was a power she'd never known she'd had. She had daydreams of maiming, of hurting them, but this was real. This was *vengeance.*

"Not so fucking pretty now, are we?" Pam asked.

The crowd gasped and *the cunts* looked back at her, bat in hand, with a grin on her face.

Coach Braun was trying to calm the injured girl, but even he stopped when Pam spoke.

"Go get the fucking nurse!" he yelled, spit flying from his mouth. His eyes were wide with panic. "Tell her to get a fucking ambulance, now!"

Pam dropped the bat and gave him a mock salute using the brim of her batting helmet. She dropped it in the dirt, knowing she'd never need it again. Slowly, admiring the beauty of the spring day, Pam made her way back to the school to get help.

Chapter 8

Pam showed up to work a half hour late. The elevator doors opened and she walked into the office like it was nothing. She kept her eyes forward and moved straight to her desk. Every eye in the room followed her.

It wasn't only her tardiness, but her appearance. She was always put together: hair, makeup, clothes, accessories; but not that day. Pam wore an old pair of slacks that were a size too small. Her little bit of belly fat bulged over the edges of the straining material. The shirt she wore wasn't much better. It was an old sweater that had more than a few pulls in it. Her hair was pulled back into a bumpy ponytail and there wasn't a speck of makeup on her face. Over the last few days her skin had gotten worse and even more oily. Pimples grew, most red and angry, but a few were tipped with white-heads, full to bursting.

Pam plopped into her chair and glared at the stack of paper in her inbox.

"Pam?" a voice asked, standing to the side of

her desk. "Are you okay?"

She turned and looked, seeing Tamara standing there. Pam blinked, as if trying to find her focus.

"I'm still a little under the weather," Pam mumbled, but managed to smile. The lines around her mouth seemed to deepen, especially without any makeup or concealer.

"I'll say," Tamara blurted out. "You look like hell. Maybe you should've stayed home another day to rest up." Tamara took a step back, as if just realizing her friend was ill.

Pam shook her head. "Nah, I'll be ok. Just have to push through it." She turned her head back towards the stack of papers and grabbed the first of many off the top.

Tamara gave her friend a final glance and walked away. Whatever Pam had, she didn't want, that was for sure.

Pam's fingers, now chewed to the quick, meandered around the keyboard. She hit the backspace button more than anything.

The smell of *Joy Baccarat* nearly made Pam vomit. Her hands clenched and unclenched, wishing for something sharp.

Denise stood next to her cubicle. Fucking Denise. The perfect little obedient wife, skank bitch. The choir girl with the heart of gold, an ass to kill for, and the most perfect set of tits known to man.

Pam's nostrils flared in anger and rage,

allowing more of the perfume to flood her senses. She closed her eyes, squeezing them shut with such force she saw stars. Her fingers dug into the keys, nearly to the breaking point. Everything had a breaking point.

"Pammy, are you okay?" Denise asked in a little girl voice. It sounded sweet and innocent, but Pam knew better. She knew those words dripped poison. They were full of malice and torture.

Pam's fingers quivered and she opened her eyes. Starbursts faded from her vision, but floated around like photo negatives. She didn't look at Denise. She couldn't. She knew if she did it would be bad. It would end in bloodshed. The thoughts of Ashley's destroyed face from that day on the softball field rushed back into her mind. She could see her in the dirt, writhing in pain. The physical pain was exquisite for Pam to see, but the pain of disfigurement, of a *pretty girl* being made ugly was even better.

"Pammy?" Denise asked again, stepping closer. She had to know she was being ignored at this point. She couldn't be that stupid. "You don't look so good." Denise made a motion to rub Pam's back, but stopped, thinking better of it. Her coworker wasn't looking just sick, but agitated. Almost feral. "I have some astringent wipes for your…your," Denise was going to say 'pimples', but didn't. "Your skin."

Pam still hadn't turned, or acknowledged her. She typed, slowly and methodically, striking each key with force.

"Anyway, if you need them, you know where to find me." Denise left, but her scent lingered.

The odor of the perfume enraged her. The sound of Denise's voice incensed her. Just being in the room with the catty cunts made her want to get a shotgun and have at it. The fear and screaming of them all trying to hide as she stalked them down and destroyed them with the gun. The smell of their piss, shit and perfume as the acrid odor of gunpowder filled the room. It would be heavenly.

And then, for the topper, was the voice of Dr. DiBiro, playing on repeat.

You're sick. You need help and I can't give that to you.

Sick.

Sick.

Sick.

I'm not fucking sick. I'm just fine. My only request is beauty. Is that so fucking hard? Is that too much to ask?

To. Just. Be. Beautiful.

Pam's mind raced and her vision was starting to fade. She'd never passed out before, but thought she might. She stood, feeling every eye snap to her. She didn't look at them.

Fucking cunts! she thought, but wanted to scream.

Pam grabbed her purse and walked to the

elevator.

Mr. Rosamilia intercepted her. "Pam, are you okay?" he asked, catching her as she hit the button for the lobby.

Pam blinked, long and slow and turned her head. Her grin, the maniacal one she'd seen in the mirror, was back.

"I thought I was better, but I'm just not feeling it," she reached out and touched his arm.

Normally, her pervy boss would've relished in a touch from the fairer sex. Not this time.

Mr. Rosamilia looked at her hand. He stared at her chewed fingers like they were snakes. When she took her hand away, he brushed at his suit jacket, as if he could remove her touch.

The doors opened and Pam stepped in. She turned around, looking at the eyes watching her. She stared back, unblinking, unflinching.

The doors closed and Pam began her descent.

Her apartment was dark. The only light was the one above the stove, which she never turned off. Pam sat on the couch, wearing a hoodie.

After coming home from work, she picked up her cellphone. She stared at the last number that had called her: Dr. DiBiro's. She stared at it and seethed. Her finger hovered over the *send* button, begging her to push it. Willing her to push it.

It was a mistake, she thought. *He was just testing me, seeing if I am loyal and worthy of his gifts. To make sure I wouldn't come screaming for help. He needs to know I'm stable. He needs to know I'm ready. He'll call back, I fucking know it.*

He didn't. The hours ticked by and still her phone didn't ring. Pam held it, willing it to ring, praying for it to ring, but its silence mocked her.

Finally, night had fallen. She didn't mind the darkness; it was the best concealer.

Pam's mind raced, thinking back to work. To the stares and condescending remarks and the fucking hissing. They didn't know she heard it, but she did. She heard them hissing and chatting and gossiping.

...like shit. Ugh, I'd never show my face.

...her nails. What is she a child?

...good thing she covered her saggy tits with that sweatshirt. No one should have to see them.

They didn't think she could hear them, but she did. Their comments were low, but Pam knew how to listen. How to pick things out from the din of the conversation. The mutter and jumble of words. No, she was smarter than that. She knew. But the worst, the worst cunt of them all? Fucking Denise.

That fucking cunt offered me face wipes? Like I'm in 7th fucking grade.

Pam was a live wire, shaking on the couch.

She needed to move, to stretch, to do something. Anything before she caught fire.

She stood, feeling the stiffness in her knees and back. She walked over to the sink and filled a glass with water.

"I'll take a walk," she said to herself, water dribbling down her chin. "Yeah, a nice, brisk walk. Take in the night sights of the city." Another sip and more dribbles. Pam slammed the cup on the counter, sloshing the remaining water out. She noticed something else, something that seemed like it was in another life: the box cutter. The one she'd used to open her last package of beauty supplies. The blade still peeked out from the plastic body. It was angled and glistened in the light from the stove.

Pam picked it up and brought it up to her face. The smoothness of the steel. The hint of sharpness. How could something so small and delicate lay flesh open so wide? A temptation washed over her, but only for a second.

What would this feel like slicing into me? When I get my surgery, will my unconscious body remember? Will it remember the penetration of cold steel into warm flesh? Like a rape of metal. Pushing into me, the meat of my body fighting to not be entered, but finally succumbing to the steel.

Pam put the blade against her cheek, just barely touching it to her skin. Even though she wasn't cut, she could sense the sharpness. With a *snap,* she retracted the knife back into the plastic housing.

Pam stuffed it into her pocket. She needed to get out of her apartment and the night was calling to her.

Pam walked; to where, she didn't know, but she walked.

It was cold out, but the wind had died down, so it was bearable. Not that she cared. The tempest inside of her blew hot and kept her warm. Pam's hood was up and her head was down. She played with the box cutter in the large, front pocket, exposing and retracting the blade. Her other hand would touch the razor's edge, tempting it to slice her. The slightest amount of pressure, just under the threshold of bloodshed, was applied and then removed.

The city wasn't too busy, at least where she was. She didn't know the time, but knew it was late. The foot traffic was light, nearly non-existent, and the cars weren't clogging the streets. It seemed like everyone was avoiding her. Like she was a pariah.

Pam walked, the box cutter dance continuing...and then she heard it. It was faint, but she heard it.

"Ugh, she's gross."

It was light, like a specter on a breeze, but

it was there. Pam's ears perked up and her blood pressure began to rise. She raised her head, seeking the source.

There weren't many options and she quickly found a trio of young women outside of a bar. They were fumbling with lighters, shivering in the cold. They were dressed similar, in different levels of sluttiness, ranging from miniskirts, to low-cut shirts. Their makeup was caked on and not in a nice way. In a way of inexperience, not knowing what true beauty meant.

Beauty. Wasted on the young and dumb.

Pam slowed down, but continued to walk towards them. Her grip on the box cutter tightened.

"Yeah, that fucking slut," a girl said, pausing to take a drag of her cigarette. "She looks like a fucking bum." The other two laughed. Their cigarettes smoldering in their hands as they listened to their friend's vulgar story.

Pam kept moving, closer, so close...and stopped. The one on the left, the one she couldn't quite see from the beginning, turned. It was Denise. No, not Denise, but damn, it could be her fucking sister. Her pulse pounded, threatening to destroy her blood vessels.

Even bitches that look like Denise laugh at me. The pretty girls. Too many pretty girls.

Pam walked, moving with a purpose this time.

Too many pretty girls, that's why I don't get

noticed. Ashley found out what happens to pretty girls who become monsters. The sound of the softball crushing the girl's face came to Pam like a welcomed friend from the past.

Still, the laughter from the group of young women grated on her nerves. Her frayed and damaged psyche. *They think I'm the ugly one? Fucking cunts. That's why they laugh at me. Well, let's see if this is funny.*

Pam entered their little smoking group, her hands still in the front pocket. The razor was extended, ready to slice.

"Ah, can I help you?" The Denise look-alike asked, furrowing her brows at the intruder.

Pam had never hurt anyone before, at least intentionally. She'd claimed what happened to Ashely was an accident, just a well-hit ball. Part of her thought that was true, but deep down she wanted to hurt her. She focused on the girl's face when that pitch came. Pam conjured up the years of abuse and torment at the hands of *the cunts* and their queen bitch.

This was different. This was a cold-blooded attack on an innocent woman. A woman whose only crime was being beautiful and looking like Denise. Pam had a moment of hesitation, but then it all hit her again. The feeling of superiority over Ashley. The look of her once pretty face, twisted into a bloody and crooked mess. That power over another person, to make them into a monster. The laughter of the women still rattled around her mind, bouncing and bruising everything it touched. Pam clenched the razor even harder and her hand shot out of the hoodie in a blur.

Pam looked up at the girl's face, guiding the razor.

She aimed for her eye.

Pam's razor hit the girl in the forehead, just above her left eyebrow. The thin steel made short work of the flesh, scraping against the dense bone. It slid effortlessly through the girl's eyeball, which popped and oozed. The girl's cheek was flayed open, revealing her molars. Finally, it skipped off her jaw bone, ending the path of destruction.

Pam was in slow motion. The world came to a near stop and she felt alive. The alien feeling of cutting human flesh felt so natural to her. The release of ocular fluid and slicing the membrane was like nothing she'd ever felt. And the macabre smile the girl had given her when she revealed her back teeth through a sliced cheek was surreal. Pam wanted to stay, wanted to watch the girl bleed. Wanted to watch Denise bleed, but she couldn't. It was that day on the softball field all over again. When Coach Braun told her to go and get help, she had to fight to follow his order. She wanted to watch, to see the carnage and suffering. To see what she'd created.

Not so pretty now, are you? she thought, watching the flap of skin hanging from the girl's face.

A scream, one of intense pain, burst from

the girl's pouty lips.

It was like a starter pistol for Pam. The scream, the blood, the smell of cigarette smoke and perfume, it all snapped her back to reality. She retracted the bloody blade, stuffed it into her pocket, and ran.

No one chased her.

Chapter 9

Pam stopped going to work. She didn't even bother calling in; they knew she was sick.

She woke up the next morning feeling reborn, like a bear coming out of hibernation, or a butterfly emerging from the cocoon. Pam sat up and stretched, reaching for the ceiling. It was one of those good stretches, the kind after a long day or hard workout. She felt like she'd achieved something, but her brain was slow to fire. Until she saw her hand.

Brown blood lined the creases in her knuckles and was under her chewed up nails. The memory of the girl, the girl who *used to* look like Denise, came flooding back to her.

Pam smiled and fell back into her plush bed.

"The look on her face…" she said, trailing off with that grin. Pam put her hands on her cheeks in almost a surprised way. The smell of dried blood was faint, but more than noticeable. Her heart was racing again, like she was reliving the scene. The phantom feeling of the blade cutting young flesh came back to her, almost as if the knife was in her hand.

"No, I didn't kill her," she said aloud, "but now she'll know what it's like to be ugly. To be *normal*, to be a regular person with scars and deformities." The grin widened further, deepening the creases in her face. "They'll say, '*Oh, you used to be such a pretty girl*,' and she'll cry and run away to hide her monstrosity of a face." Pam began laughing. Not hard, but it was enough to make things jiggle.

She stopped, looking down at her sagging breasts. They hung low, drooping from either side of her chest. Pam reached down and lifted her shirt. She stared in disgust.

Her breasts were an abomination. They looked like fleshy bananas, topped with veiny, pink nipples. Those nipples that were still sore from the shower. She fucking hated them. The bane of her existence. She grabbed them, forcing them back up onto her chest, not in her armpits. She squeezed them, but just enough to make them look full and firm. The way they should look.

Pam let them drop and sighed. She hadn't heard from Dr. DiBiro and didn't think she would. Not after the other day. He wasn't the man she thought he was, that was for sure.

Pam would've stayed in bed the entire day, but her bladder said otherwise. She pulled her shirt down, hiding her shame, and walked into the bathroom.

A monster stared back at her in the mirror. Pam froze, almost not recognizing herself.

Most people don't look amazing when they roll out of bed, but Pam was not ready for what awaited her. Her skin was a mess, with new pimples, angry and red. The old ones from the day before were capped with white heads. They glistened with pus, begging to be popped. The bags under her eyes were dark and heavy. They hung from her face, so much so, that she could actually lift them. The patches of her skin that weren't blossoming with pimples were dry.

Pam knew she looked like shit. The mirror didn't lie. *But what was the real problem?* She stared at her reflection, this thought rolling around her head, like dice in a cup. *The pretty girls are the problem. They take all the attention. I used to be pretty, but I deserve to be beautiful. I need to be beautiful.* In her current state, Pam knew she was far from beautiful. Then, it hit her. The attack on the Denise-looking girl. She was a pretty girl at the start of the night and now she was a disfigured freak.

Pam smiled again. *If there are less pretty girls in the world, then I'll get more attention. I'll help raise up those girls like me. The average who strive for beauty. I'll flatten the curve of beauty. And when I become beautiful, no one will be able to ignore me. No one.*

Pam touched her reflection in the mirror, her fingers leaving small streaks of dried blood. It was a face she didn't recognize. But she knew it was her own. Her true self.

Pam had to go to the hardware store, but first she needed a shower.

Alicia pulled the backdoor of the restaurant closed. She turned the key and gave the handle a tug, ensuring it was locked. She hated closing up after a dinner shift, but her promotion to assistant manager didn't give her much choice. Until she could move up in seniority, and get the lunch shift, she was stuck.

She gave the door another yank, just for her own self-assurance. She put the keys back into her purse and wrapped her hands around a small can.

Alicia pulled a can of pepper spray, a gift from her father, from her purse and stuck it into her jacket pocket. It was a chilly night and the wind off the river didn't make it much better. She zipped her jacket and stuck her hands inside of the warm pockets.

She hadn't lived in the city for a long time, but heard all of the horror stories, mainly from her father. Young girls being assaulted or raped. Well, not her. If they tried, they'd get a face-full of pepper and a kick in the balls. Alicia wasn't going to be another statistic in the growing violence.

She started her walk towards her

apartment, which was only a few blocks away. Her eyes were always on alert for any perverts lurking around. She wanted to pull her cellphone out and check her social media in the worst way, but knew it was a distraction. Nope, she stayed ever vigilant, watching. Then, she saw the person. Alicia felt her heart racing as someone wearing a hoodie began walking towards her.

Alicia squeezed the can of spray tight in her pocket, with her thumb hovering over the button.

The streetlights were far apart, but Alicia thought it might be a woman coming towards her. She relaxed, just a little. A woman probably wouldn't rape her, but they could still rob you.

The shadowy woman stopped just outside of the streetlight.

"Oh, thank God, another woman," she said to Alicia. Her voice sounded sweet.

Alicia relaxed and even smiled a little.

"Is everything okay?" Alicia asked, stepping forward into the darkness.

"It's better now that I've found you," the woman responded. "I got into a fight with my boyfriend and he threw me out on the side of the road. I'm not from here and am just looking for a bus stop. I'm sick of his shit and I'm going home."

Alicia, only twenty-four years old, had been in her fair share of shitty relationships. She felt like she'd found a kindred spirit. She even felt bad for considering pepper spraying this woman.

"I wouldn't have bothered you, but my

fucking phone died," the woman said, the nasally sound of crying permeating her voice.

"Awe, it's okay," Alicia said. She'd been there and knew women needed to stick together. After her last relationship, she was seriously considering becoming a lesbian. "Let me look it up for you." She took out her cellphone, lighting up her face.

Her beautiful face.

It was too easy. Too much fun. Too brutal.

Pam had never heard of muriatic acid until only a few hours earlier. It was a version of hydrochloric, that was slightly diluted. It wasn't the skin melting solution like she'd seen in the movies, but it would do the trick.

Finding her victim was almost as easy. The city, especially the east side, was full of nice restaurants and bars. Pam simply ducked into each one until she found a target. A target that looked like Denise. If anything, there were too many beautiful people for her to narrow it down. That would soon change. Soon, she'd look like them. They'd all be on the same playing field.

Pam waited in the shadows outside of the restaurant, watching. Finally, her time came.

The young woman was confident, alert, not playing with her phone. Pam knew she'd have her work cut out for her. She decided to play the 'sister-hood of the broken hearted' card. When the woman softened thanks to Pam's excellent acting skills, she knew she had her. It was just a matter of time before she was able to strike, blinding those beautiful eyes and burning that soft skin. When the woman went for her cellphone, Pam knew it was time.

"Awe, it's okay," the young woman said, pulling her cellphone out.

Pam grinned in the darkness and adjusted the small container of acid in her hoodie pocket. She didn't dare unscrew it yet, but her hand was poised to do so.

The light of the cellphone lit up the woman's face, giving Pam a perfect target. She pulled the container from her pocket and unscrewed the lid.

"It says here the bus stop is only three blocks away." The woman kept scrolling, not knowing what awaited her. "I'll walk with you, if you'd like."

Pam struck. The acid flew from her hand, splashing in the woman's face.

Pam watched as she blinked; that momentary pause before your pain receptors lit up in Defcon 1. The screams were next.

"What the fuck!" the woman shrieked. Her voice sounded rough, like she'd spent a night smoking and drinking. Or it could've been the acid burning her throat. She stumbled back into the light of the streetlamp, her hands clawing at her face.

Pam smiled in joy. She followed her into the light, watching her work unfold.

The acid wasn't movie strength, but it sure did the trick. Angry blisters formed on once pristine skin. The woman's eyes were squeezed shut, but a pink slime ran from any crevice it could. Her breathing was ragged and she began to cough.

Pam took it all in, that plastic grin never fading.

The woman, blinded now, clutched at her throat and fell to the ground. Her knees hit the asphalt hard, splitting her jeans and exposing blood. She coughed harder, and each breath came with a struggled wheeze. Another cough, but this was wet.

Pam stepped back as the woman began hacking up bloody mucus.

Her coughs sounded like she'd breathed in broken glass. They were wet, deep and rough, each one worse than the one before it. The coughs began to slow and the ones that slipped out were wheezy and forced.

The woman fell to her side, and this time the breathing was even shallower. She pulled at her throat, as if willing air to pass the swollen and burned corridor of her windpipe. Her short nails dug into her flesh, ripping furrows of blood and meat. Anything for another breath.

Pam watched in glee. Another beauty down, and she took a step higher in the world.

The woman, still fighting for her life, found the energy to force her eyes open.

Pam stared at the milky white eyes blindly gazing at her. She could see the plea for help, the questioning glance and...the disgust. Even in her imminent death, the beautiful woman looked down on Pam. Her ruined eyes glared at her pimples and dry skin. They even seemed to pierce her clothing, seeking out her sagging tits and loose stomach. Pam fucking hated her, but she'd had enough.

She turned and walked away. The sound of the woman's dying struggle sounded like laughter.

Chapter 10

It felt like an eternity since Joe had seen Pam. In reality, it was only days. He may not have seen her physically, but she lived in his mind. Day and night, she was there. Invading his thoughts. Haunting his dreams. When he saw the first attack, the disfiguring of the young woman, he had a gut feeling he knew who the culprit was. The acid attack sealed the deal.

Pam. She was erasing beauty from the city, one young woman after another.

Joe had the TV on, but it was low. He didn't need to hear it; he already knew the stories. If it wasn't Pam hurting and killing, it was someone else. Some other person killed or maimed. Or another hardship. The world was full of horrors, but he, he had made beauty. No longer. Not in a world so black. Not when society said he was wrong, or he was sick in the head. Yes, he had a few particular *perversions*, but what a small price to pay for art. For the art of the flesh.

Joe took the bottle of bourbon from the

end table and poured another glass. The bottle was almost empty. He felt like he'd opened it only moments earlier. A dark trip down Memory Lane would do that to a man. Especially if Memory Lane was full of despair, heartache and self-loathing.

Joe drained his glass, but didn't grimace. He was too far gone to even taste the liquor. It just added to his stupor…and burrowed into his thoughts.

A photo album sat closed in front of him. It was thick and old, a fine layer of dust on the cover. The word *MEMORIES* was embossed on the faux leather. He picked it up, the weight of it nearly overwhelming him.

Joe wiped the dust away, revealing another few words, these written in pen on a small paper tag.

The DiBiro Family.

Joe's eyes stung as his wrinkled hand rested on the words. When he'd first gone to prison, when his world came crashing down, he thought he'd cried his last tear. He was wrong. Countless nights he wept in his cold cell, hoping the other inmates didn't hear. They did. At least he figured they did. He could hear them, whether it was crying, begging, praying or masturbating, he could hear it all. Joe spent every waking moment waiting for a visit. That special moment when an officer would come in and tell him he had visitors. That day never came. Day in and day out, Joe would wait, like a stray dog waiting for an adoption. Joe wasn't led to lethal injection, like a dog, but many days he wished he was dead. The days melted into weeks, months and years. The only thing he'd received was divorce papers, but that was it.

When Joe was released from his cage, he looked for his family. He wished he never had. His wife was promptly re-married, to a lawyer of all things. She and his two sons moved away, running from the shame he'd brought on them. The pain and embarrassment of having a sicko as a father and husband. His boys, his only children, wouldn't talk to him. Even as grown men, with families of their own, they disregarded him like a pariah.

Joe felt tears running down his face as he opened the photo album. It felt forbidden. A time long ago when he'd been happy, when they'd all been happy. Page after page, he turned, reliving some of the best times of his life. Times he'd never get back. Times he was doomed to remember until the end of his days.

The end of his fucking days was coming soon.

Joe flipped through. He could feel the sun on his cheeks when he stared at a beach picture. The firmness of his wife's rump as he grabbed her during a Christmas photo. The taste of a Fourth of July hotdog and cold beer as he manned the grill.

Joe cried. No, he sobbed...hard. The cries wracked his body, causing his chest to heave. His fingers touched the faces of his boys, who might as well have been ghosts. He tried to remember their voices. Those little voices they would've had in the pictures.

He slammed the album shut and grabbed the bottle. Joe put it to his lips and drank. Bourbon spilled from his mouth, but he kept sucking it down. His throat burned, but it burned good. Like the fires of Hell. Like the penance he deserved.

Joe pulled the bottle from his face and took a deep breath. His crying had slowed. He wiped snot from his upper lip with the back of his hand. The two days' worth of stubble made a raspy sound against his flesh. Joe palmed both eyes, pushing the tears away. He took a deep breath and grabbed the gun.

It was small and would be an instant parole violation if he was caught with it, but Joe didn't care. When he was released from prison, he was afraid. Afraid of the world, afraid of who might be coming for him. Afraid of what would happen to him if his past was revealed. He knew it was a bad idea, but he needed it. Being caught with it was a sure-fire way to have his parole revoked and land him back in prison for the rest of his life, but he didn't care.

The day never came when he needed the gun. No one gave a shit who he was or what he'd done, but still, the gun was his safety net. Until then. At that point it was a way out. A way out of the fucked up mess he'd created.

Joe opened the cylinder on the revolver, confirming each chamber had a live round in it.

They all did. He snapped it shut with a flick of his wrist. Joe's vision wavered; the last chug of alcohol was hitting him hard. He pointed the gun at his face, staring into the dark maw of the barrel. It was short, dark and finite, ending with the top of the hollow point bullet.

How will I look after this bullet takes my head off? Will it hurt? Will my head be gone, or just a little hole? That hollow point is supposed to open up inside of me, gathering my flesh, bone and brain.

The gun wavered in his outstretched hand. He wouldn't be able to shoot himself in that position. It was too awkward and he was too drunk. He'd probably miss and shoot himself in the ear. Then he'd need a plastic surgeon.

The thought of death didn't bother him. He'd been ready to die since his first day in prison. Or maybe when his wife served him. Either way, he didn't fucking care. No, it wasn't death; it was wasted talent that scared him. His gift. His gifted hands, which held a weapon of death, they would be useless. As the bullet tore through his brain, all the years of schooling and experience, the little techniques he'd picked up over the ages would be gone.

Joe put the gun in his mouth. He stuck his tongue in the muzzle, tasting old gun powder and cleaning solvent. He closed his eyes.

All of that talent, gone, he thought with his thumb on the hammer. His breathing was ragged and quivering. Slowly, he began to pull the hammer back. Millimeter by millimeter, it crept. With a loud *click*, it snapped into place. It was one of the loudest sounds he'd ever heard. That was it. Now was the time. Just a few pounds of pressure on the trigger and it would all be over. No more thinking about his wife getting fucked by some pussy attorney. Or his sons calling that man Dad. Or grandchildren he'd never hold or bounce on his knee. His pain and torment would be a splatter of gore on the wall. He would rot in his chair until the decaying smell of his putrid flesh alerted a neighbor. The police would come and find his soupy corpse, nearly liquefied in the chair, a gaping hole in the back of his skull.

All that knowledge. All of those gifts…gone.

No, he couldn't. Not yet. He needed to see the pictures one last time.

Joe pulled the gun from his mouth; the bitter aftertaste remained. He snatched the bottle and took a sip, washing it away. Joe set the gun down and grabbed a photo album. This one didn't say *MEMORIES*. No, it didn't say anything at all. This was his, his personal trophy collection.

Joe opened it.

Augmented breasts, lipo-suctioned thighs, re-shaped noses. His name carved in flesh. His cock in the mouths of the unknowing. His cum, the first shot of spunk on a new set of perfect tits. Tiny slivers of metal hidden in wounds. A gloved finger in an anus. They were his trophies. Those were the memories he would live in forever. If only he could create more. One last hurrah before his dance with death.

Pam.

That crazy fucking bitch, running wild, maiming girls to make herself look more beautiful. No, she was too much. Too wild. Too unpredictable. But what was life without a little craziness? His mind wandered back to the feeling of his cock in an unconscious mouth. The danger in that when he'd go into recovery and play with them. Knowing that he could be caught. It drove him. It fueled his perversion. It was something he thought died in prison. He was wrong.

Joe put the photo album down and picked up his cellphone.

Pam sat in the darkness. She couldn't stand looking at herself any longer. Her beauty was fading, melting into nothingness. With each pretty face she carved up, burned or maimed, fifteen others took over. There was no way out. She knew it now. She knew her time was coming to an end and sooner or later, she'd be caught. Part of her didn't care. What was the point of living if you were mundane? If you didn't turn heads on the street or hear the whispers of jealousy. Was life worth living if you were ugly?

The darkness told no lies. It didn't show a

disgusting face in the mirror. Or reveal folds of loose skin or veiny nipples. There were no ingrown pubic hairs, now swollen and topped with whiteheads. The darkness knew her. The darkness made her feel beautiful.

Pam stunk. She could smell her body odor and it was offensive. She didn't care. It smelled almost animalistic and that's what she was, an animal.

The last girl, one she just left bleeding on the street, had pissed herself. The first cut of the blade, the sight of her flesh and blood, made her lose her faculties. Pam sliced and cut, relishing the feel of the knife gliding through human meat. It left Pam feeling intoxicated, but now she was hungover. She was hungover from the violence. But mainly from the futility of her quest. She might as well try to drain the ocean.

Pam stared ahead. Something was lighting up, disrupting her blanket of darkness. It was shrill and piercing. Pam looked down at her cellphone as it rang. The number wasn't saved, but it was one she knew. Her heart raced. She picked it up, the vibrations feeling in sync with her beating heart. Pam's finger hovered over the 'accept' button.

Why? Why now? Why would he call me? He already told me to fuck off. That he couldn't—no, wouldn't—help me. If he can't make me beautiful, who can?

Her mind raced, a million thoughts

bouncing off each other. The phone rang again, the vibrations felt angry. Screaming at her to answer.

Pam touched the green button.

"Hello," she said, her hand shaking as she put the phone to her ear. She began sweating. Not the sweat of exertion, but fear.

Nothing. Not a sound. Maybe, just maybe, she heard breathing. Pam didn't pull the phone away to check the connection; she knew he was there.

"Do you want to be beautiful?" he whispered.

Pam thought she was going to puke. Her heart was thudding and felt out of rhythm. "Yes, more than you know."

"What are you willing to pay?"

"Everything." She felt like she was in a dream. She was a disembodied head floating in the ether, watching the exchange.

"What are you willing to do?"

Pam froze. She knew the answer. She'd always known the answer. The fact her mind didn't hesitate made her uneasy. She'd already gone so far.

"Anything," Pam said. She hadn't realized she was holding her breath.

Silence.

Then, the line went dead.

Chapter 11

Latham Park, where they'd first talked about surgery. Where the idea to do the unspeakable—harvest implants from another woman— was born. It was again the location of a meeting, this one much more sinister.

Pam sat on the same bench, bundled up against the wind. The weather had been getting worse, the temperature dropping. She sat protected from the wind, but mainly against the world. She felt like the caterpillar, wrapped in her cocoon, waiting to be reborn. But, unlike the butterfly, she'd be transformed in flesh. In flesh and saline.

Joe walked over to her, his gait slow and meandering.

Pam watched him from the shadow of her hoodie. She thought he may have been drunk, but didn't really care. As long as he was sober for the grab and surgery.

His eyes were down, as if avoiding the wind gusts, but it was calm at that moment. No, he didn't want to look at Pam. Not yet.

Joe sat down next to her, pulled his hands from his pockets and blew into them.

"Weather's pretty shitty," he grumbled, yanking his coat tighter. He still hadn't made eye contact with her.

They sat in silence for a moment, neither knowing how to go about the next part. Finally, Pam spoke.

"So, when can we do this? I've been pretty rough lately and could really use this now."

Joe ran his tongue along the inside of his cheeks. He fished something out of his teeth, which was odd considering he hadn't eaten yet. It was sour and bitter. He spat, realizing it was an errant chunk of vomit from the night before. He shivered, not from the cold, but from revulsion.

"Did you bring the money?" Joe asked, turning to look at Pam. She was secreted in her hood, but he could see enough.

The once beautiful woman was a shell of herself. Her face looked sallow and gaunt. Pimples littered her cheeks and black bags hung from her eyes. Her eyes were droopy, yet had a maniacal sheen to them. He never would've guessed a person could fall so hard in only a few days. Then again, he did look in the mirror that morning.

Pam reached into her pocket; she'd stopped carrying her purse.

"Yes, here it is. Everything I own is in this envelope," she handed him a plain envelope of cash. It wasn't bursting, but it should be enough. It had to be enough.

Joe took it, a little discouraged about the thickness, and quickly put it away.

"It should be enough. I still know a few people who operate on the fringes of their oath, so hopefully this will work." Joe couldn't get his hands on implants or other prosthetics, but he was hoping to at least get some anesthesia. A few doses would be more than enough for his plan, if everything worked.

Pam smiled an unsettling smile. She looked like a rotten pumpkin someone had carved into a Jack O' Lantern.

"Great, I have the address. When can we do it?"

Joe knew it was wrong. He felt it in his bones. This was it for him, his last and best masterpiece. He'd show the world he was the best of the best, no matter what anyone said. Who else could perform such a surgery? No one. Not a single person he'd ever met would even have the balls to do what he was going to do. It was wrong, but fuck, did it feel right.

"In a few days, possibly tomorrow if I can get everything right away," he said, the thoughts of his creations fluttering through his head.

Pam sighed, but knew that moving that night was a pipe dream. She didn't know how long she could wait, but then again, beauty wasn't something to rush. Beauty took time and patience.

It took getting up hours early to perfect your makeup, hair and nails. It took hours in the gym and diet, to get rid of just a few pounds of fat. All the while you continued to age and watch your skin droop and wrinkle. And then, with all the hard work, some little cunt would come skipping in with smooth skin, wide eyes, tight waist, a round ass and a perfect chest. She would flaunt it, showing off how beautiful she was. She would put you down at every available opportunity, not even knowing what she was doing. What a fucking lie! She knew; they all knew. When they saw her on the street, they'd whisper. Or in the back of the office, when she'd order the burger and not a salad, they'd laugh. At the makeup counter, when she'd be in desperation mode to find the concealer or cream that would soften lines, they'd mock. Well, no more. The fucking joke was on them. Pam *would* be beautiful. She would turn heads and the whispers would be of jealousy, not disgust. Especially with the amount of disfigured women running around.

Joe looked at her, afraid of what was going on in her head. Pam was staring off, not focusing on anything, just staring. Her face was split in that grin, the one he'd only seen a few times, but still brought unease.

"Okay, I'll be in touch," Joe said, hoping to break her reverie.

Pam shook her head, as if shaking off a bad dream.

"What?" she asked.

Joe adjusted his coat, patting the envelope of money just to be sure. "I said I'll be in touch." He was getting ready to walk away and stopped. Another thought, maybe it was a warning, popped into his head. "Oh, and Pam," he waited for her to acknowledge him.

"Hmm," she looked up.

"You might want to stop your nightly..." he was at a loss for words. *Your nightly terror runs, you fucking crazy bitch,* he thought and wanted to say aloud, but didn't. "Your nightly...escapades."

Pam feigned ignorance, but did it poorly. "What are you talking about?"

Joe leaned closer to her, getting a whiff of body odor. "I watched the news, Pam. The girls. The pretty girls. Leave them alone. I can't help you if you're in prison."

Pam smiled. It was so genuine and sick. "Yes, daddy." The baby talk was repulsive.

Joe shivered, turned and began walking.

Pam watched him shuffle away. She knew hurting pretty girls didn't make her better looking, but it was oh so much fun.

Pam stood up to leave. She had a date. A date with a box cutter.

Chapter 12

Monica knew he was trouble the moment she laid eyes on him. She knew it even more when he walked over to her, the scent of his cologne following him like a sexual specter. Of course, she accepted his free drink; she would've taken one from an ugly guy, but from a hottie, it was a no brainer. The flirting was casual at first, she flipping her hair and making a production of sucking her straw, he, with downtrodden eyes, looking up at her. She imagined he'd look the same way if he was going down on her.

Monica slid her bar stool closer to him, feigning like she was having trouble hearing, but they both knew differently. No, she wanted to be closer to him, to smell him, for him to smell her. They were both animals and the mating dance was in full effect. Monica uncrossed and crossed her legs, catching him glance down at the inviting mound under her skirt. She'd opted for a red thong that night, which even in the dim lighting gave him a little show.

"See something you like, Peter?" Monica asked, not breaking eye contact as she nearly deep-throated the straw.

Peter felt himself swelling and wanted to adjust his growing erection, but if she wanted to show off, he would too.

"Maybe," he said, sipping from his drink. He couldn't believe she was in the bar alone or that no one else was hitting on her. She had a rich head of auburn hair and piercing blue eyes, something Peter hadn't seen very often. Her body was a thing of beauty too. Her skirt hugged wide hips, and a thick ass. Not to mention, her blouse was filled out nicely. Peter smiled and put his hand on her thigh.

The heat from their combined flesh was like an inferno.

Monica licked her lips at his touch, and willed his hand to go higher. To explore her. Slowly and ever so slightly, she opened her legs.

Peter was young, only in his early twenties, but he wasn't dumb. He could take a hint and slid his hand up her thigh.

Monica was wet. She was horny when the night began, hoping to get laid by someone attractive, but this was nearly insane. In her college years, which were only a few years removed, she'd done some daring stuff, but hadn't been fingered in a bar. She opened her legs even further, not caring who could see.

Peter's fingers grazed the lace of her underwear. He knew he had her; he could feel her warmth through the fabric. Gently, he teased her panty line, touching the flesh.

Monica was vibrating with lust and the fact he was teasing her made it even worse. She wanted to crawl up on the bar and get fucked right then and there. Or at least jam his fingers into her.

Peter pulled the lace away, revealing her bald vagina. It was smooth, so he figured it was freshly waxed. He ran a fingertip through her slit, which was practically drooling. His cock was full to bursting, and he didn't know if the teasing was worse on him or her.

Monica was nearly lost in her passion, even after being bumped by another bar patron. That bump jarred her attention, bringing her eyes south...to Peter's jeans. What she saw contained in that denim prison made her shudder.

She leaned in, welcoming Peter's fingers to explore her further, deeper. They did. Monica bit her lip, but maintained her composure as he rubbed her from the inside.

"Do you want to take this outside?" she asked. One-night-stands weren't her thing, but she hadn't had a good lay in a while. Plus, Peter was hot and clearly packing.

Peter nuzzled her ear, "I thought you'd never ask." Reluctantly he removed his fingers from her. He threw $20 on the bar and helped Monica into her coat.

"Shall we?" he offered his arm, as she adjusted her thong.

"We shall," she replied, smiling and letting him lead her out.

Pam stood in the cold, watching, waiting. The bar scene of the downtown was her new hunting grounds. She knew it was risky, especially being so close to her goal, but she couldn't help it. Seeing them, the beautiful girls no longer beautiful, was in itself a thing of beauty. To watch clear, clean skin part beneath her blade, or blister from the acid was almost as rewarding as being beautiful herself. Pam couldn't rid the world of them all, but each one was one less she'd have to compete with.

The side door of the bar, the one leading to the alley, burst open. A couple spilled out into the dimly lit corridor, their mouths locked together. Pam knew their tongues wouldn't be the only things exposed that night. She grinned and opened the box cutter in her hoodie. She closed it with an audible *click* and began her stalk towards them.

The sound of fucking echoed down the alley. It wasn't an unfamiliar sound to Pam, but one she hadn't heard in a while. The young couple were really having at each other, and she could just see them in the gloom.

The woman was against the wall, with

her hands bracing herself so her face didn't get smashed into the brick. Her face. Her beautiful face. In the low-light, Pam could see her delicate features. The firmness of a youthful ass, which was currently exposed. Her male counterpart was equally as picturesque, as he bucked against her hips.

Pam took a step closer. Her face was bathed in shadow as she stalked them. They didn't even notice.

"Holy shit," the guy said, "I'm gonna cum." He increased his rhythm and his stroke depth.

The churning of bodily fluids intensified.

"No, not yet," the woman moaned, taking one hand off the wall and putting it between her legs. "Just hold out or fucking slow down," she begged, feverishly rubbing herself, hoping to achieve her release before her partner.

"Oh fuck," he moaned, pushing deeper.

"No, no, not inside of me," the woman said in a panic, her lust seeming to die as her lover deposited his load into her pussy. She pushed back, trying to get him out of her, but his hands were on her hips, keeping him deep.

He smiled, pushing himself to the base. "Oh, come on, just get the morning after pill." He relaxed a little, giving her the chance to push him away. His cock slid out of her, a glob of semen drooling from his piss slit.

"I told you not to cum in me," the woman shrieked, her hand, which was once being used for pleasure, now catching globs of his spunk.

"Oh, you did?" He smiled, his cock still out, glistening in the dim light. "My bad." He grabbed his still erect member and shook it in her direction. "This little—well, kinda big—fella has a mind of his own." His grin was repulsive.

Pam had seen enough…of both of them.

She stepped forward, knowing they still didn't detect her. With her left hand she reached out and grabbed his sticky, hard cock.

"What the fuck?" The man jumped as a strange, cold hand wrapped around his member.

Pam hadn't had a penis in her hand in quite a while, but she knew this was a pretty damn big one. She didn't think the box cutter would take it off completely, but it would do more than enough. Pam pulled her other hand from her hoodie pocket, making sure the blade was fully extended from the plastic housing. In the dim light she could see where the base of his shaft met his pubic hair. It was the perfect target.

The blade made short work of the tendon supporting his erection. It snapped like she'd cut a wire. Steel carved through the spongy flesh of his cock, bathing her hand in blood. Pam yanked, hoping to get it to break free, but the blade wasn't long enough.

"Fuck!" the man screamed, pulling himself away from her. His hands cupped his mangled and dangling manhood, which was pouring blood. He tripped on his pants, around his ankles, and fell into a puddle of filth.

"Hey, what the fuck are you doing?" the woman asked, not fully seeing what'd happened. She was looking at her date lying on the alley floor cupping his crotch. The low-light must've disguised the blood.

Pam smiled at the woman. The woman she'd just saved. The woman she'd avenged. The beautiful woman who wouldn't smile back at her. Pam's smile wavered as the distraught woman flailed her arms at her.

"I can handle myself," she pointed to the man bleeding out on the ground. "It was under control. You didn't have to hit him in the nuts."

Pam could smell her cheap perfume. She could smell the sex juice and cum on the woman's hand. But she could see. Oh, she could see that beautiful face, with the blue eyes and auburn hair. And she could see her disgust. The disgust the woman felt looking at Pam. At her skin, her clothes and her body. Pam's stomach roiled and she didn't feel like smiling anymore.

"You fucking crazy bitch!" the woman spat, trying to push past Pam to check on her date, who was whimpering.

Pam reached out and grabbed the woman's hair. Her bony hand wrapped tight in the perfect locks and pulled.

"Hey, fuck off!" The woman tried to turn, but felt something in her mouth. Something sharp.

Pam jammed the blade into the corner of the woman's mouth, feeling it twitch as she spoke. The skin of the cheek was delicate, as she'd come to learn.

Oh, you don't want to smile at me? Well, this should help, she thought.

Pam sliced, feeling the flesh yield to her blade. The edge skipped off the woman's molars and careened towards her thin neck. Pam didn't care, she only wanted to feel the meat flay open under her knife. Muscle and blood vessels gave way to the intruding razor in a bubble of gore. A canyon of red opened in pale flesh, quickly filling with blood.

The woman gagged and coughed as her windpipe was severed. A wet hacking sound erupted from her useless neck. Her hands flailed, clawing at her throat, trying in vain to seal the wound. Fighting for a breath that wasn't full of gore. She gurgled and started to go limp. Each attempt was weaker and weaker as the life dripped out of her one bloody bubble at a time.

Pam's hand was already covered with penile blood, but now it was soaked. The woman went limp in her arms, falling to the ground.

Pam's heart was racing. She looked around for witnesses, but the cold night kept prying eyes away. She closed the box cutter and put it back into her pocket. She tucked her bloody sleeve as deep as she could into the hoodie and walked away with a grin on her face.

Joe rubbed his hands in front of the heating vent of the Cadillac. The plush leather seat was warm too, something vehicles didn't have when he went to prison. At least, no vehicle he'd ever owned.

"A bit nippy out there," Joe said, looking at the man in the driver's seat. "The walk didn't help much..." he trailed off, hoping his former colleague would offer him a ride home.

Alvin Gleidman sat in the driver's seat of his new Escalade, watching a man who he'd once revered, warm his hands like a homeless person at a burning barrel.

"Yeah, well, sorry Joe, but that's not happening." He looked around the area, but the old commuter lot was empty. Had been for years. "But I really can't be seen with you and not to mention, what we're doing isn't quite legal."

Joe took his hands away from the blessed heat, happy to have feeling back in them. He smiled.

"Since when did you care about legality?" Joe gave a small laugh, making a dribble of snot run down his stubbled upper lip. He absently wiped it with the back of his hand.

Alvin looked at him with contempt, but

knew he was right.

Alvin fucked more prostitutes and did more cocaine than anyone he knew. That was illegal, but not terrible. He had other vices though. Bigger vices with dangerous people. Alvin loved dog fighting. Not the actual training of the dogs, but watching and betting on it. The sound of the yelps and yips from the dogs, the screaming of fans, the smell of death and blood. It excited him. But Alvin was like a black cloud. His bets almost always lost and even though he made a lot of money, he'd fallen in debt with some dangerous people. Dangerous people who knew where he lived. He cared for his personal safety, of course, but when he received a picture of his daughter and granddaughter outside of their house, he knew something had to be done. His debts needed to be paid and paid in full, or they'd be paid in blood.

"Here," Alvin said, pulling a paper bag from his coat pocket. "It's all there, but I'm not sure what you need that much Propofol for."

Joe opened the bag and pulled out a few glass vials of the anesthetic. A handful of syringes accompanied the drug as well, saving him a trip to the store. Satisfied, he closed the bag and reached into his own pocket.

"Here," he handed Alvin the envelope with the cash.

Alvin's eyes lit up at seeing the money. He opened the flap, and thumbed through the bills. Another chunk of debt repaid. Satisfied, he stuffed the money into his pocket.

"Okay, I wish I could say it's been a pleasure, but I'm not a liar," Alvin said.

Joe sucked at his teeth, making a low hiss.

"Yeah, well," he patted the bag in his pocket, "nice seeing you too." He opened the door and held on as a cold gust threatened to pull it from his grasp. Without looking back, he slammed it, muttering, "Fuck you," under his breath.

The big SUV sped away into the darkness.

Joe bundled his coat tight, his hand holding the bag. There was still more to do, but this was a step in the right direction. A step towards his greatest challenge, and his greatest masterpiece.

Chapter 13

Joe read and re-read the text message over and over. His finger hovered over 'send' for what seemed like an eternity. He knew that pressing the green button would be it. Any chance he had of getting out of this whole mess would be lost forever.

His mouth was a desert, begging for a drink. Not of water, but of sweet alcohol. He wouldn't, not until the message had been sent. He needed to be sober for what was to come.

Joe swallowed, his parched throat clicking. He pressed 'send.'

Pam heard her phone go off. The TV was low and she didn't even know what was on. The dull blue of the screen was the only light and when her phone beeped and lit up, she jumped.

For the first time in a long time, she was clean. The blood of the couple she'd carved up dried on her skin. It was sticky and crackled, and wholly made her uncomfortable. It wasn't the act of slicing them—no, that was fun—but the feeling of blood. Dried blood.

When she'd come home, she took a quick shower. Then she bagged up her hoodie and tossed it in a dumpster. It was her favorite, but she knew it had to go. There was no way she was going to get caught when she was so close to her goal.

To beauty.

The box cutter was easier. That she took apart, soaked in hot water and dish soap and wiped it down with bleach.

Pam sat on the couch...and waited. Her mind raced and calmed, fading to almost nothing. She would snap her eyes up to the TV, forgetting it was on, and stare. She didn't watch, but stared. Stared at the beautiful people. Their perfect teeth. Blemish free skin. Tight bodies. Full chests. She stared and seethed.

Pam picked up the phone and looked over the text message. It was an address and nothing else.

She typed back.

Now?

A text bubble popped up. Dr. DiBiro was writing. Pam took a deep breath, willing herself to calm down.

Yes.

Pam read it over and over, memorizing the address and figuring out her bus route. It was getting late, but she didn't mind. Beauty didn't have a bed time.

The coffee was cold and untouched. Pam picked at the chipped ceramic with an equally chipped nail. She looked into the blackness of the drink, seeing her own distorted reflection staring back.

"It could work," Joe said, breaking the silence that hung in the air.

Pam broke her gaze, leaving her reflection drowning in the dark coffee. She looked up at the doctor. They'd only met a few days ago, but he appeared to have aged years. Pam didn't look much better, her reflection made that quite clear. But that would soon change. Once she had a perfect set of breasts, things would change. She'd improve her diet, bringing her skin back to its glory. The gym would be the perfect place to show off her new set of tits, thus helping her shed some unwanted pounds. Denise, who, if she survived the surgery, would be so ashamed she would quit. Pam could saunter back into her job, probably landing a promotion. She knew Mr. Rosamilia would give her a pass, especially with her new *assets*. They just had to follow the plan.

The plan, something they'd spent the last two hours discussing, started off in the weeds.

The more and more they discussed it, the better it became. What started as a sadistic pipe-dream, was one step closer.

Pam didn't answer. She didn't know if she needed to. She picked up her cup and sipped the cold coffee, grimacing at the bitterness.

"It will work," she whispered into the cup, looking at Joe over the rim. She set the cup down, watching the ripples dance.

Joe nodded, running the plan over in his head. There were a lot of variables, but he felt like they could be negated. They had to be negated.

"When?" he asked, staring at her.

Pam could feel his gaze, even though she was still watching her coffee. As if being physically pulled, she looked up.

They locked eyes, their minds seeming to link in the moment. Fear, fear and desire were drawn in expressions.

"Tomorrow." She clenched her fists and then extended her fingers to the sound of cracking joints.

Joe nodded. "Okay, I'll make sure to get the van." He sipped from his coffee, which he didn't mind cold. "Thank God they never installed those cameras in the lot."

He always figured it was for the insurance money, but Joe thought it was odd his employer didn't keep their rental vans under surveillance. He was thankful for their lack of caring, that was for sure.

Pam took a deep breath. "Okay, tomorrow night."

Joe removed a piece of paper from his pocket and slid it across to her.

"We'll need some supplies before we start," he said, taking another sip.

Pam unfolded the paper and nodded. She hoped her credit card wasn't too close to the max. "Fine," she refolded the paper and stuck it in her pants pocket.

Joe knew her answer before he asked, but needed to anyway.

"Are you sure?" He looked at her, waiting for her to finish with the paper.

Pam rubbed her pocket and licked her chapped lips. She was sure. She'd never been more sure.

"Yes. I'll do anything to be beautiful."

Joe simply nodded.

Chapter 14

Denise sat on the couch watching some trashy TV show. She knew it was rotting her brain, but Bradley was on his computer and not ready to watch their normal show. Until he was ready, she'd watch drivel on the massive flat screen.

Denise curled up, tucking her legs underneath. A wool blanket kept her toasty and comfortable. She reached over to the end table and grabbed her glass of wine. She sipped and replaced it. Her hand snaked back out, lithe and graceful, delving into the bowl of low-calorie puffs. They were essentially flavored air, but she liked them. Well, she liked them *enough* and it kept her away from the real junk food.

Foxy, her little mutt, sat at the bottom of the couch, begging. Her tail wagged, almost in sync with her panting tongue.

"No, go lay down, Foxy," Denise said, popping a puff in her mouth. The flavor was like a flash in the pan and dissolved almost instantly.

The dog continued her begging, this time

with a little whining added in.

Denise sighed. She grabbed a puff and held it down for the little dog.

"Here, but don't tell Daddy," Denise whispered, as if Foxy had any intentions of being a tattletale.

Foxy inhaled the morsel, licking her chops as she did.

"You aren't feeding the dog those stupid puffs, are you?" Bradley asked from the other room.

"Shit," Denise muttered. "Ah, no," she said back to him. "One fell and the little beast grabbed it before I could pick it up." It was a weak lie, but if Bradley wanted to get laid, he'd let it suffice.

"Sure," he said, a touch of sarcasm in his response. "You should walk her soon. You know people food doesn't agree with her stomach."

Denise rolled her eyes, but she knew her husband was right.

A few weeks ago, she'd given Foxy a couple potato chips and the dog had the shits for two days. It was a nightmare having to clean up after her. Luckily, Foxy was only 22 lbs, so her turds weren't too big, but it was still annoying.

A gust of wind picked and opportune time to blow, rattling the window panes. Denise shivered at the thought of going outside. She needed to turn on the charm and hoped Bradley was feeling generous.

"Hey, babe?" she cooed, almost moaning.

She knew his hot buttons and a little moaning could go a long way.

"Hmm," he grunted from the other room.

Fuck, she thought. *If he's not even answering with words, I'm probably fucked.*

"Do you think you could take her out? I'm so warm and it would be a shame if I cooled off. You know how long it takes for me to heat back up." She turned around and knelt on the couch. Denise rested her arms on the back of the furniture, looking towards the office her husband was in. The door was open and she could just see the side of his head. She tugged her tank top down, revealing more of her expensive cleavage. Hopefully, he'd look her way and get an eyeful, and his little head would convince his big head to take care of the dog.

"I guess I can," he said, but didn't look at her. The sound of the keyboard clacking was almost aggressive. "But it might not be for a little while. I'm almost done with this report and don't want to stop now." Bradley kept typing. "Can she wait?"

As if on cue, Foxy let out a hellacious fart. Nothing chunky, but it was a prelude of what was to come.

"Don't worry about it," Denise sighed, throwing the blanket off her lap. She stood up, looking down at the dog. "Come on, you little shit machine."

Foxy's tail hadn't stopped wagging and she knew it was time to go outside. She ran over to her leash by the door and began jumping.

"Don't let her shit on the floor," Bradley added, the typing stopped for the moment.

"Don't let her shit on the floor," Denise mocked, just low enough for only her to hear. She threw on her heavy coat, a pair of boots and hooked Foxy up on the retractable leash.

Denise stepped out into the cold night. The streetlight by her door was out, which was odd. If it had been working, she would've seen the van. The van with the covered logo of the hardware store.

Pam felt like a cop on a stakeout. She and Joe sat in the van, waiting and watching. It felt like an eternity, but it had only been a few hours, if that. They parked under an unlit streetlight, which was a stroke of good luck. Another stroke of luck was the lack of occupied buildings next to Denise's. Gentrification had struck again, driving out most tenants in the area. The surrounding buildings, of which there was only a few, were under construction and presumably vacant.

Dr. DiBiro had picked her up in the van he'd swiped from work. It was a normal, run of the mill panel van, with a sliding door. The only issue was the logo of the hardware store on the side. A few sheets of whiteboard and duct tape made short work of the signage and blended nicely with the paint.

The heat was on low in the van, but Pam was still sweating. She had been ever since he came to pick her up. She was really going to do it. She was finally going to be beautiful.

Joe picked at a nail, which was already short. He hissed when it went too low.

"Fuck," he put his finger in his mouth and sucked the little droplet of blood.

Pam didn't budge. She just kept staring at Denise's door, willing it to open.

Come on, you fucking cunt. Just get your fucking ass outside, so we can get this show on the road. Pam's mind was a tempest, raging against her skull.

There. Movement from inside the house. Someone was up and walking around in front of the windows. Someone tall and appearing to be feminine.

Pam held her breath and swatted at Joe. She did it blindly, not wanting to take her eyes off the door.

"What?" Joe asked, annoyed, with his finger still in his mouth. He turned his attention over to the front door. He could see a shape moving inside. It was her. His stomach flipped and he thought he was going to shit, puke or possibly both. Joe took a shuddering deep breath. "Ready?" he asked. His foot hovered over the brake, preparing to put the van into gear.

Pam watched the door open. It was her.

Denise. The fucking cunt and her little dog too. She pulled the mask, an old-school ski mask, over her face.

"I'm so fucking ready."

Joe pulled his mask on and felt like he was on auto pilot. It was surreal, the entire week or so. Before he'd met Pam, he was worthless, a nothing-being floating in the waste of the world, just waiting to die. Now, he was back. His talent, his magic was alive again. The chance to make body art was rekindled.

Joe tapped the brakes and put the van in gear.

Denise pulled her jacket tight, fighting off another blustery gust.

"Come on," she said, stamping her cold feet.

Foxy sniffed, squatted and let out a little dribble of pee. No poop, not yet. The cold didn't bother her, unlike most small dogs. She was fluffy and finally not panting. Nope, this was her kind of weather and she was going to take her time. Foxy pulled Denise away from the front door.

"Pick a fucking spot and shit already," Denise muttered. Foxy looked at her, licked her chops and continued sniffing.

The sound of a vehicle drew Denise's attention, but she didn't see any headlights. She squinted, as if that would help her see any better.

"What the fuck?" she said, watching the white van heading towards her. "Look at this dipshit," she said to Foxy, who was starting to circle a thin patch of grass. "They don't even have their lights on."

The van slowed and pulled over, stopping right in front of Denise.

A cold, creeping fear stole her breath. It wasn't the same cold as the air, but a bitterness that cut her to the bone. The occupants were wearing masks. This wasn't uncommon in the winter, but the passenger's eyes. They possessed a coldness like no other.

"Can I help you?" Denise asked, backing away from the person who exited the van. She tugged Foxy, who was mid-shit. She looked to both of them; the driver had also exited and was approaching her on the other side. The passenger held a zip-tie in their hand, which wasn't much of a threat, but the driver, the driver held something much more sinister: a needle.

Denise continued to back away, keeping her eyes on the pursuers. They didn't speak, but they moved almost as one. Her free hand felt behind her, hoping to find the railing for the steps. She didn't dare turn around.

"Get the fuck away from me," Denise ordered, but the pair still advanced, this time even faster. She was suddenly very hot; the fear was an inferno in her chest. Her eyes darted from one to another. Denise stepped again, trying to put more distance between her and them. She stumbled and felt herself going down.

The pair didn't waste the opportunity and moved in.

Denise hit the ground hard, her teeth clicking together. Foxy yipped as she was pulled through the air towards her owner. Denise put her hand down, trying to push herself up to get back to her feet, but they were fast.

"No! Fuck you!" she yelled and kicked at the person with the needle. "Bradley!" Denise screamed.

The pair looked at each other, panic in their eyes. Their plan, whatever it had been, was falling apart. Denise just had to get her husband out there and chase them away.

"Scream again, and I'll fucking carve you up," the passenger said. They held the zip tie in one hand and in the other was a box cutter. The industrial tool looked menacing in the gloom, the edge telling her its secrets in the dark.

Denise's eyes left the person with the needle and had gone wide at the sight of the blade. Not only the sight of the blade, but there was something familiar about the voice. She knew it, but couldn't place it. It sounded distorted, almost garbled, but feminine.

No, she couldn't stop. If she didn't yell and fight, they'd win. They'd take her and then only God knew what would happen. Denise inhaled, preparing her lungs for another ear-piercing scream, when she felt a pinch.

The needle was plunged into her neck, unleashing its payload.

"Bradley," she yelled, but not nearly as loud as before. Her brain felt like it was stuffed with cotton. She was becoming drowsy, but was still awake, at least for the time being.

Foxy circled Denise, nipping at the attackers, trying to protect her mama.

Good girl, Foxy. Give'em hell, Denise thought. Her vision was blurring and everything seemed to have trails following it.

Foxy let out a loud yelp of pain and then she was quiet.

Denise watched as the passenger grabbed her wrists and began wrapping them up with the zip tie.

"Hey, what the fuck is going on out here?" Bradley yelled from the door.

Pam hurt her toe when she kicked the dog, but the little fucker kept biting at her. The fat little thing weighed more than she expected, but when she felt its throat collapse under her shoe, she knew it was down for the count.

"Tie her up and let's get her in the van," Joe said, capping the exposed needle. He'd only given

Denise half the dose. They needed her to be able to stand in order to get her in the van. Carrying dead weight was not easy, especially in a rush.

Pam put the razor away and wrapped Denise's wrists in the zip tie. The plan was working, but not nearly as smoothly as she'd hoped. She had her back to the building and heard Joe open the sliding door on the van.

"Hey, what the fuck is going on out here?"

Pam pulled the zip tie, hearing each of the teeth click as it tightened. She jumped at the booming voice.

"Denise? What the fuck did you do to my wife?" Bradley, who Pam had recognized from the pictures on Denise's desk, asked, moving down the steps.

Fuck, Pam thought, watching the man jog down towards her. He wasn't big, but he was young and in shape. There was no way she'd be able to take him out with the box cutter, not without ambushing, which was off the table.

No, I was so fucking close! Pam's mind screamed, willing the man to turn away. To leave them alone. To not ruin her one chance at beauty.

The streetlight, the one that was black, began to flicker to life. The scene in front of Pam danced like a movie reel.

Bradley wore a white dress shirt that was partially open at his throat. His Clark Kent haircut was messy, but in an intentional way and his square jaw was flexed in concern. The concern melted to anger when he saw his wife drugged and bound. He didn't even notice the corpse of Foxy laying nearby.

Pam had never been punched by a man, but it sure looked like that was about to change. The fear she had seen in the eyes of Denise, just moments earlier, was plastered to her masked face. She fumbled for the box cutter, hoping to keep him away.

Thunder and lightning exploded from the clear sky. Except it didn't come from the sky, it came from the van.

Bradley stopped short, and looked at his shirt. A small hole, about the size of a .38 caliber bullet, magically appeared. A crimson bloom began to spread, staining his white shirt. The thunder boomed three more times. More holes and much more gore.

Pam turned, her ears ringing, and looked at Joe with the smoking revolver in his hand. In the distance, like they were miles away, someone was yelling. Gunshots would bring onlookers, but no one would interfere beyond yelling. At least she'd hoped. The internal clock was ticking in her brain, knowing the cops would be called. This wasn't the shitty section of the city where gunshots were a normal thing. Pam only hoped the license plates and decals had been covered well enough.

Bradley fell, clutching his chest and stomach, but very much alive. His life blood was pumping through claw-like fingers. The other hand reached towards Denise, who might as well have been on the moon.

Joe stepped out of the back of the van and walked over to the wounded man. He stood over him and looked down in the flickering streetlight.

Perfect cheekbones, clear skin, straight nose and bloody, yet straight teeth. A waste, he thought.

Joe raised the gun, and watched the man hyperventilate, forcing more blood from his throat. A bubble of gore popped, running down the fatally wounded man's chin. Joe cocked the hammer…and fired.

The bullet hit Bradley just under the left eye, the overpressure forcing it from the socket. It didn't come out completely, but was left bulging, with a corona of blood. A patch of Bradley's all-American haircut was flapped over. The chunk of his skull that was in the path of the hollow-point bullet had burst, taking a sliver of scalp with it. Slowly and with a finality of death, Bradley's hands fell, landing on the sidewalk in a growing pool of blood.

"Get her in the van. Now!" Joe tucked the warm gun into his pants pocket and motioned for Pam to help Denise into the vehicle.

Denise was still conscious, but barely. The gunshots helped keep her awake, but the drug was doing its job a little too well.

Without ceremony, they tossed her into the back of the van and re-took their seats.

Joe put it in drive and drove off.

Pam ripped her mask from her face and smiled. She looked back at Denise, who was drifting in and out of consciousness. She knew the woman was defenseless, but she stared at her anyway. Not to ensure she was awake or not, but to gaze upon her perfect set of breasts.

Joe drove in silence. The only sounds in the van were the breathing of both women. Denise had finally succumb to the drugs, but that was okay. He'd be able to wake her enough to get her into the apartment, at least he'd hoped. He wasn't as strong as he used to be.

The warmth of the gun, which had since cooled, still remained. The phantom heat was nauseating against his leg. It felt alive. Maybe it was the life force of the Clark Kent man he'd just killed.

Killed. Joe had killed a man. Not only that, but he'd killed him in cold blood. Not for the noble sense of self-defense against another armed opponent, but for his own volitions. He squeezed the steering wheel, careful not to let his emotions run into the accelerator. The last thing he needed was to be pulled over. Once they'd cleared the small neighborhood, Joe stripped the poster board from the decals and license plate. He knew the cops would be looking for a plain, white van. He hoped the disguised vehicle had been good enough to throw off the witnesses, if there were any. He had come so far, too far, to let something silly like an observant cop stop him now.

The image of the man's face distorting as the bullet entered played back in Joe's mind, like a cruel movie. He felt the gun buck, spitting death into a perfect face. The man's family wouldn't even get to have an open casket.

Joe pulled up to the back of his apartment building. The service elevator stood closed, but he'd long since swiped a key from the maintenance office. He was certainly full of surprises.

The van rolled to a halt, the tires crunching on small pebbles. Joe killed the lights and engine, but neither he nor Pam, moved.

The sound of breathing…and moaning.

"Braaaaaddddlleey," Denise groaned from the floor of the van.

"Fuck," Pam said, pulling her mask back over her face.

Joe did the same, but with less haste. The drugged-up woman didn't know him and even if she saw his face, she'd never remember. When they dump her in the park after the surgery, she'd be lucky to survive, let alone ID any of her attackers.

"Come on, let's get her in the elevator," Joe said, opening the driver's door.

Pam took a deep breath, letting the chemical smell of the cheap mask calm her. It was almost time. Just a few more steps.

Chapter 15

Pam and Joe were panting as they laid Denise on the folding table. It was a sturdy, old wooden one, but was well worth it. The table had been lined with heavy plastic, along with the floor around the surgery area. A second one, that one reserved for Pam, was next to it.

Joe's apartment wasn't very large, but it was more than enough for what he'd need.

He grabbed a small IV bag and attached it to a standing coat rack. It had been filled with the remaining anesthetic, diluted in a bag of saline. He placed it near Denise and ran the line to her hand. Gently, he inserted the needle, then pushed the plastic catheter into her vein and retracted the needle, hooking up the IV, knocking her out completely.

Pam breathed a sigh of relief. She was winded from helping the drugged woman through the halls. Once she'd recovered from the surgery, her gym routine would begin again. Then she'd be in shape; much better shape.

Joe grabbed a bottle of bourbon off the counter and poured a generous amount into a dirty cup. He chugged it down and re-filled it.

Pam walked over to him.

"Do you think that's a good idea, considering you have a double surgery on your hands?"

Joe let the bourbon sit in his mouth. He stared at Pam, tempted to spit it into her eyes. But he didn't. He swallowed without grimacing and offered the bottle to her.

Pam looked at it.

"What the fuck," she said, grabbing it by the neck. She drank, coughed and drank again. "Well, let's fucking do this." Pam handed him the bottle back, releasing it before he had a grasp. It hit the ground, but didn't break. She walked over to Denise's still form.

Even after the traumatic episode she'd just faced, Denise was beautiful. Not from creams, or makeup or even her implants, but she had a natural beauty about her, something money couldn't buy.

Pam never hated a person as much as she hated Denise in that instant. Not even Ashely and the other *cunts*. No, this was something else, something deep-seeded and visceral.

I think I hate you more than I hate myself, she thought.

"Your fucking husband is dead," Pam whispered into her ear. Even that was delicate and perfect. "You hear me in there, cunt? Your fucking Bradley, the man of your fucking dreams is dead. He has a fucking bullet in his brain. Oh, and that yappy little fucking dog? Dead too. I watched her gasp for her last breaths after I gave her the boot." Pam was grinning now. A wide grin. A thin line of drool ran from the center of her mouth, landing on Denise's open jacket.

Joe watched, and took another sip of bourbon. The bottle was almost empty and none had spilled out when it fell. He set it in the sink and walked over to the women.

"Help me undress her, so we can do this," he said, making sure he kept his distance. He wasn't sure how Pam would react if she were startled.

Pam's head turned slowly, the grin, the drool, all still there. The plastic smile wavered and her lips twitched.

"Fine, let's do it."

They began to undress Denise, cutting off most of her clothes with surgical sheers. Until finally, she was completely nude.

Pam stared at her in abject horror.

Denise was perfect. Even more so than Pam expected. Her breasts were works of modern art. Even on her back, Denise's tits barely hung, but they did. They drifted towards her sides, but not too much. Just enough to look natural. When Pam laid down without a shirt, her breasts were practically on the bed next to her. If they were a little bigger, they would be.

Denise's skin was tight with youth and a sense of athleticism. Her stomach was flat and had just the hint of muscle tone. It was nearly blemish free, except for a tiny birthmark next to her belly-button, but even Pam thought it looked cute.

Pam's eyes continued south, taking in the shape of Denise's hips. They were wide and Pam knew they led to a perfect ass on the back end. The pelvic bones stuck out just a little, but that only brought her eyes to her hairless mound. Denise's pubic area was bald and not just shaved, but probably lasered. There wasn't a hair on her, which made Pam feel uncomfortable, like she was looking at a large child. Even her vagina was neat, and perfectly closed up. Pam's wasn't a mess, but a real woman had pussy lips.

Denise's thighs, tight, toned and perfect. Her lower legs had not an ingrown hair or patch of stubble.

Pam wanted to vomit. This level of beauty, of absolute perfection, was nearly impossible. This was a woman that belonged on the cover of a magazine, the magazines she'd based her life on since she was a little girl. Seeing them... everywhere. The perfection, the happy smiles, the clear skin. Every. Fucking. One. They all had secrets, but they wouldn't tell. No, they wouldn't help you, not completely. If they did then the world would be full of supermodels and not 'Pams.' No help, just shame.

...lose 10lbs this weekend...

...how to get your dream guy...

...oily skin? 5 steps to a better you...

...the top 10 push-up bras and why you need them...

Pam's fingers reached out, as if she was in a dream. She hesitated before resting them on Denise's warm, smooth skin, like she was touching a live wire, not a woman. *Not a fucking hair, or stubble to be found,* she thought as she placed her hand on the woman's leg. She ran it up and over her knee. *Nope, smooth as a baby's ass.* Her fingers split, going on either side of Denise's vagina, riding the contours of her outer lips. *Fucking perfect.* Pam felt out-of-body, like she was watching from afar. Watching a sculptor with clay crafting a woman from mud. Pam's fingers danced over the flat stomach and had arrived. Arrived at the reason they were all there: Denise's chest.

Pam's heart was racing. *What if they didn't feel good? What if the looks were deceiving and they were hard as rocks? No, stupid, you've felt them pressed against you. When this little cunt would hug you. She did it on purpose, to show you, for her to flaunt them. For you to know you'd never have them. For you to know you'd never have a young hunk of a husband, who'd fuck your brains out and blast his load on your big, fake tits. No, she did this to you to torture you. Fucking squeeze them! Fucking feel your new life in front of you!*

Joe watched Pam's hands linger over Denise's chest. Her face was a mask of turmoil.

Whatever was going on in her head seemed like an eternal struggle. The twitching in her muscles, the clenching and unclenching of her fingers and the grin. That fucking grin. Most women smiled, usually something coy or delicate. Even when they're laughing a big belly laugh, they look feminine. Not Pam. No, that fucking grin was like a clown mask. Like Jack Nicholson as the Joker, but without the makeup.

Pam's hands cupped Denise's breasts, lifting them slightly.

"Oh my god," she whispered.

Joe stepped forward, hoping nothing had gone wrong. "What is it?" He looked down at the supine woman who was currently being fondled.

Pam squeezed Denise's breasts, making her hard nipples jut out. She looked at Joe with tears in her eyes.

"They're perfect," she chuckled. "They're absolutely perfect." She brought her attention back to Denise. "You are perfect, but not for very long," Pam said to her face. The unconscious woman didn't move. Pam pinched Denise's nipples in-between her forefinger and thumb, holding her breasts up with the pink flesh. "Your perfect life is over," she laughed, pinching her nipples harder. "Your beauty is done, your life is over and you'll wallow in misery for the rest of your pathetic existence." The tears were gone, but the laughter was not. Denise's nipples were turning an angry shade of red, bordering on purple. Pam brought her face closer to Denise's, almost nose to nose. "No. More. Miss. Perfect."

Joe took a step forward, his hand raised, but Pam released her clasp on Denise's breasts and turned.

"Cut her fucking tits out," Pam ordered.

Joe had his hand up and was nodding. "Yes, that's why we're here, but we need to prepare and do it quickly." He looked at the IV bag attached to Denise. "I don't have an unlimited supply of that and if you'd like your procedure under anesthesia, I suggest we hurry this along."

Pam didn't say anything, just stared. "Cut her fucking tits out. I need to see them, to feel them."

Joe sighed. He wasn't getting anywhere with Pam, he knew that.

Denise grumbled. "Brrraaaaddddllleeeyy."

Joe and Pam snapped their heads to the woman.

"Hey, what the fuck?" asked Pam, who took a step back, worried Denise was going to jump up at her.

Joe adjusted the IV and Denise stilled. "That's what I was trying to get at. Without a ventilator, I can't really put either of you completely under. You might stop breathing," he looked back at Denise to ensure just that. "This is the best I can do without a surgical suite or team."

Pam licked her chapped lips. The roughness of her skin felt good against her tongue.

"Cut her fucking tits out and let's get this show on the road."

Joe didn't argue. "Fine, I'll go wash up."

Pam stared at Denise. She drank her in, wanting to be one of the last people to see her this way: perfect.

Joe was back in minutes and he carried a small metal tray of tools. He picked up a purple marker and uncapped it.

"Do you mind?" he asked Pam, motioning her to step back. She did and he began prodding Denise's breasts with his fingers.

Pam watched as he touched the other woman. He drew lines and markings, none of which she knew anything of, but had seen plenty of times on the internet. He moved his head around, seemingly looking for the best light. Joe gave it another once over and was satisfied.

"Ok, now for the fun part," he put the marker down and picked up a scalpel. His gloved fingers adjusted against the metal, ensuring he had the perfect grip.

Joe's heart fluttered. He hadn't held a scalpel in years and he was afraid his hand would tremble. It didn't. It was strong and firm, still and calm. A wave of euphoria rose over him once again. He was going to make art and not only that, but in the worst of conditions. No one else, not his fucking quack co-workers, would have the balls or insanity to pull off such an operation.

Pam watched with bated breath, trying to

stay out of the light.

Joe held Denise's right breast and brought the blade to the purple line. For a moment, he didn't think anything had happened and then the flesh parted. A wrinkled line of yellow fat and blood greeted him like an old friend and he smiled.

Pam watched, knowing she'd be under the blade soon. She could feel it in her chest, the cold steel slicing her open, opening her up for the world to see. Like so many of the women she'd opened with her razor, only this time it would be for beauty, not to erase it. Ridding her of her imperfections and replacing them with a new chance at life. At beauty.

Joe worked quickly and his years of training and experience were on full display. He replaced the scalpel with another tool, this one to lift the flesh from the implant. Back and forth, he grabbed different instruments, which were usually handed to him by his team. He didn't need a team; he was an artist and this was to be his masterpiece.

One implant was out and had the remnants of fat and blood still lingering. There wasn't much, considering these were only implanted recently.

Pam stared as Joe set it on the tray. It didn't look like much, just a bag of fluid, but to her it might as well have been a diamond. She longed to touch it, to squeeze it, but she'd wait. She wanted both.

"Okay, first one down," Joe said, moving to the other side of the table.

Denise's eyes were fluttering. Her youth was fighting the weakened anesthesia.

"Braaddddddlllleeeyy," she moaned.

"Fucking fuck," Joe stammered, looking at the remaining anesthesia. A bead of sweat rolled down his forehead. "This isn't going to work." His heart was racing, not from the thrill of surgery, but for the fact he might fail. He looked at Pam, who was at his side. "If I give her more drugs, there won't be enough for you. Not only that, but what I do have might not keep her out long enough to get her stitched up and out of here." He stepped back and took a shuddering breath. "No, we're so close." He adjusted the IV again, noticing how low the diluted drug was getting.

Pam could've wept.

No, no, no! Not this close. It can't be possible. Her mind was in turmoil. In the beginning, she thought this was a pipe dream, something a crazy person would think of. But, as it moved closer and closer and the plan evolved, she thought it could work. Now, in the moment of truth, when they'd come so far and spilled so much blood, the thought of failure was unbearable.

*So much blood,...*she thought and smiled. *What's a little more.*

Pam left Joe's side as the doctor began to size up his next incision.

Joe was sweating. The stress, the warmth, the pressure, it was finally getting to him. He'd been a top doctor in the world and now he was floundering for a simple explant surgery. Alvin, that little fuck, would be laughing his ass off right then.

Joe's brain was cloudy. It could've been the alcohol, but he'd performed surgery much more fucked up than he was at this point. No, it was the failure. Even though he was performing a surgery in his tiny apartment on old tables, with minimal equipment and no help, he still expected to succeed.

It didn't matter; he'd continue until there was no hope. Every passing second brought that line closer and closer.

He could see Pam out of the corner of his eye, although he tried to focus on the task at hand. She was on the verge of tears; her mind seemed to be fighting itself, as if trying to figure out a solution. When she walked away, he wanted to look, but he had an idea where she was headed.

The knife hissed when she pulled it from the butcher's block.

"Ah!" Pam yelled, pushing Joe out of the way. She raised the knife in both hands, high over her head, lining up the tip with the center of Denise's chest.

Please don't hit the implant, Joe thought. *What a cruel fate that would be.*

He could've stopped her, could've told her the whole thing wasn't worth it, but he would've been lying to himself.

The blade descended with a *whoosh* and entered Denise's chest, narrowly missing the remaining breast.

Denise's eyes flew open. The searing pain from her heart being impaled tore her from the grasp of weakened anesthesia. She tried to sit up, but was pinned to the table. Blood bubbled from her mouth as her eyes looked for salvation. There would be none.

Joe watched. The women locked eyes and the realization of who her captor was dawned on Denise.

She tried to speak, but her throat was full of blood. Pam must've got a lung too, and it looked like she got it good.

"Why?" Denise gurgled, still trying to sit up.

Pam looked at her, not in horror or regret, but in disgust and jealousy.

"You," she sneered through gritted teeth. "You, are no longer perfect." Pam's nostrils flared. "Your family is no longer perfect." Pam pushed harder on the handle of the knife, and deeper into the wooden table. She lowered her face, her once pretty face, to Denise's. "You are no longer a thing of beauty."

Blood didn't pour from Denise's chest, even though her heart was impaled. A steady flow came out, but the blade of the knife contained the majority of it.

Joe couldn't take his eyes off the women. His scalpel dangled from his fingers and he almost dropped it.

Slowly, much slower than he'd expected, the light faded from Denise's eyes. With a few last gasps of agonal breathing, she was gone.

Pam released the handle of the knife and ripped the IV from Denise's hand. The fluid began leaking out of the open line. Pam pinched it off until Joe could put a small clamp on the end of it. He gave her a nasty look, but knew it had to be done.

"There, now you should be good," she told him. She smiled at him with just a small splatter of blood on her cheeks.

Joe looked at the cooling corpse of Denise. The blood from her wound hadn't obscured his marks too much. He grabbed her unblemished breast and cut.

Pam slid on two rubber gloves and stuck her hands out, awaiting her prize. Her glory. Her beauty.

Joe held the implants in both hands, inspecting them for any damage. He couldn't find any and knew they were of good quality.

"Okay, not too long," he said, handing them

to Pam. "We still have a lot of work to do." He gestured his head to the body of Denise.

She looked deflated. Her one breast was expertly sliced open, ready for stitching. The other…that was a different story. After she was dead, there was no reason to worry about recovery. Joe was still a surgeon, but he moved with haste, cutting her in ways he'd never done before. His old self, the one who landed him in prison, came alive. He cut the nipple, flayed the breast and even peeled back the flesh around the impaled blade.

They were heavy, much heavier than Pam expected. They felt amazing. She squeezed them with tears in her eyes. She imagined them bouncing bra-less in a summer dress, as men ten years her junior stared in lust. Pam's dry spell would be over. She would be able to have a different cock every night. To watch them play with her, tease her, suck her. She might even let a few of them fuck her tits. To slide their cocks in between them, while she watched her beauty envelope them. And then the finish, the glistening, white semen shot across her works of art.

She knew the magazines, the billboard people, they would all be calling her. Begging her to tell her secrets. Pam would be on their covers, giving young girls bullshit answers on how to *better your body*, when it was all a fucking lie. It was a sham, the whole fucking thing. But she didn't care. No, she could bring the magazine home, and show her mother, who was still pretty. Show her what *real* beauty looked like. Pam would be the new model in the family, showing her mother what she *could've* been.

Pam sniffled, not even noticing she was crying.

Joe just stared, not wanting to know what was going on in the woman's head.

"Okay, let's get started," he said, snapping her out of her daydream.

Pam's eyes flashed with anger, and fury. The interruption of her lustful reverie almost made her snap, but then she remembered. Her mind raced back to reality and she shook off the sudden urge of violence.

"Yes, I can't wait," she let out a sigh and handed the implants back to Joe.

"Okay, take your shirt off."

Pam's cheeks reddened. No man had seen her breasts in quite a while. She had to remind herself Joe was a doctor. He was Doctor DiBiro, not Joe.

The room was warm, but when her breasts were exposed to the air, her nipples shriveled into wrinkled nubs. Her flesh bristled in goosebumps and she wanted to cross her arms over herself.

Joe grabbed a chair, careful not to drag it through the bloody plastic on the floor. He was no longer armed with the scalpel, which was being sterilized, but the purple marker.

"Let's begin."

Chapter 16

Pam was feeling sleepy. The initial shot he'd given her was a larger dose than what Denise received. The IV was hooked up to her hand and she could feel the sedative coursing through her veins. She was no longer cold, even though the plastic was quite chilly. No, she had warm thoughts in her foggy brain.

"Try to relax," Joe said, grabbing hold of her wrist. He took her pulse and stared at his watch. "You should be feeling pretty good by now." His eyes were watching the time.

Pam was feeling good. Not just from the meds but from the fact this was it. Her new life started then and there. She was ready to have all the opportunities beauty afforded. To see what was behind those doors in the elite club.

She blinked; her eyelids felt like taffy and she struggled to open them. Another blink and this time they stayed shut even longer.

"Make me beautiful," Pam said, her eyes no longer opening. Her pulse was slowing down and leveling out.

Pam's pulse was acceptable and after a couple of quick tests, Joe knew she was sedated. The bag was full enough, he hoped, to perform the surgery. He'd done hundreds, if not thousands of implant surgeries, but never one like this. He was usually in an operating room surrounded by state-of-the-art machines and nurses. It didn't matter; his skills were still sharp and he knew this.

He readied his tools, but a steady dripping was starting to irritate him. Joe didn't notice it before, but now it was almost incessant. He looked at the sink, which wasn't far away in his small apartment. Not a single drop of water fell from the dingy spout.

Drip.

Drip.

Drip.

His eyes scanned, but he knew where it was coming from: Denise.

Joe took a deep breath. He tried to push her from his mind. He tried to ignore the fact a beautiful, 20-something-year-old woman lay dead in his apartment. And for what? So a shallow bitch of a woman could have a new set of tits and he could 'work' again. Joe tried to push the image of Bradley, Denise's husband, from his mind. The young man's final act in trying to save his wife, and his final thoughts were fear and pain.

Joe closed his eyes. The only thing he could see was the deformed face of Bradley as the bullet tore into his skull.

For what?

All of it, for what?

For beauty? For vanity? For a sense of accomplishment or validity?

Joe brought his mind back to the task at hand. The reason he was there. The reason he was in the mess he was in.

Pam. The fucking monster on the table.

But, if she was a monster, what was he? She didn't force him into this. If anything, he enabled it, allowing it to progress, feeding the beasts inside of them both.

A dark, crimson gem of gore fell from Denise's nude corpse, splashing on the plastic beneath her.

It was like a starter pistol to Joe. He snapped out of his reverie and stared at Pam. Her nude breasts moved ever so slightly as she breathed. A small smile was on her face and not one of malice or hate, but happiness.

Joe had work to do. To transform Pam into what she deserved. What she always deserved.

He picked up the scalpel and began cutting.

The elevator doors dinged when the car stopped. With a *whoosh*, they parted, but Pam didn't step forward. She stayed on the car, her head turning to take in her domain. The cunts, her co-workers, stared at her in awe, a goddess delivered upon them. Delivered upon them to make them feel shame and disgust. And they should, fucking cows.

Pam stepped off the elevator, timing it perfectly, and heard collective gasps. It was as if the elevator was shielding part of her beauty. Now that she was in the light, she was nearly blinding. She knew she looked amazing, but a mirror appeared anyway, just to confirm it.

The silk of her blouse flowed like warm honey, hugging her bra-less breasts, and drifting over her mid-section. Her nipples stood erect and sensitive, kissing the smooth material. Her skin was immaculate and blemish free. It didn't even look like she was wearing makeup, but that her flesh was just perfect. Even her lips, which she licked, tasted free of anything. Pam ran her fingers through her hair, which shimmered and danced like it was alive. Toned legs, free of any razor bumps, poked out of her mini-skirt, ending in a pair of heels.

Pam walked ahead. The movement of her breasts was nearly orgasmic, the soft silk caressing them with each step.

Women groveled at her feet. Women,

hideous, plain women, wept at her beauty. Pam kept her head held high, not even wanting to sully her eyes with their mundane looks.

Her cubicle was gone, replaced by a stunning corner office surrounded by floor-to-ceiling windows. She entered and saw three nude men standing at attention, in more ways than one. They didn't look at her, but kept their gaze straight ahead. Pam walked in front of them, examining them, touching them, poking and prodding them like meat in the store. That's what they were, meat. Meat for her pleasure. For too long, women had been seen as the pleasure sex, the gender for men to have fun with. To stick their cocks in and fill up with their spunk, leaving them afterwards. No longer. Pam was the user. She'd fuck them, or make them service her, until her loins had their fill. Then, they were dismissed.

Pam had her eyes down, looking at the three erections. She knew they were all attractive, but they paled in comparison to her. No one looked like her. She was a work of art.

Pam's perfect nails grazed the shaft of a rather long cock. She ran her fingers over the smooth skin, circling the glans with her thumb and forefinger. She'd found her morning fuck.

"You, I'll take you this morning," she said, still looking at the erect penis. "But first, you'll eat this gorgeous pussy of mine until I tell you to stop. Understood?"

Pam's eyes began working their way up the

man's toned torso. A trail of dark hair led from his crotch to his chest and her eyes followed it. And stopped.

Four holes appeared in the man's unblemished skin. Four little holes. She stared at them, curiously. Then the blood came.

"What the fuck?" Pam muttered, unable to move. The bullet holes began to ooze gore. Thick, viscous blood seeped from the wounds, clumping in the man's chest hair. Her feet were practically glued to the floor as her eyes worked up to the man's face.

Bradley, Denise's husband, stared back at her. His one eye, the one that had taken the brunt of the gunshot wound, popped out. One half of his face almost looked like a frog; that bulging eye with the halo of blood around it.

"You wanna fuck?" he moaned, gun smoke slithering from his blood-flecked lips.

Pam tried to move, but her immobility seemed permanent.

"No, get the fuck away from me," she pulled at her legs, willing them to move. Suddenly, as if on a conveyer belt, she slid down to the next man.

He was pale and unflinching. His right hand held his partially severed cock.

The man from the alley, she thought, remembering the lustful couple who snuck off to fuck outside of the bar. She could still feel the release of his penile tendon in her hand.

"How about me?" he whispered through

pale lips. "You wanna ride this?" He shook his severed manhood at her. The blood vessels twitched and dripped, running down the shaft. Somehow, he was still hard. He lifted his cock back up, putting it in place. "Oh, would you look at that," he said, stroking himself now. "Blood makes the best lube." His pace quickened, gore pumping from the deep cut at the base of his penis.

Pam stared in revulsion.

Blood ran down the man's thighs, but he kept stroking. Pre-cum and blood made his shaft slick and his helmet was an angry shade of red.

"Oh fuck," he muttered, smiling at Pam.

Thick spurts of cum shot from his severed cock. The first struck Pam square in the face.

She knew it was going to happen, but her hands just weren't quick enough. The hot semen landed on her perfect skin.

Hot semen.

There was a slight sizzle before the pain. Pam heard her skin burning as the ejaculate ate through her flesh.

"Fuck!" she screamed, as she furiously wiped at the goo on her face. Strips of skin peeled off in bloody rents, as the acidic cum burned her. Liquid flesh and blood stained her nails and hands. "What the fuck did you do to me?" she screamed at the man.

He didn't respond, rather just stood there, perfectly still.

Pam tore her expensive blouse off, praying

none of the hellish semen reached her perfect breasts. She looked down and breathed a sigh of relief. Her tits were intact and beautiful. Even her face seemed to feel better just knowing her chest was still perfect.

The office door opened and her head snapped up.

"Oh, fuck," she groaned.

The doorway was full of women. Women who were young and once beautiful. Women who Pam hated. Women who Pam had mangled and murdered. Women who'd come back for *her.*

"No, get the fuck out of here!" Pam yelled, waving her blouse at them. Her feet, which had been somehow stuck the entire time, popped free. She ran behind her desk, hoping to keep a barrier between her and the ghouls.

"We want our beauty back, Pam," a woman, whose face was sliced to the bone, said. "We want it all back."

Pam pulled at the drawers, looking for something to defend herself with. They were stuck shut. Not one of them even budged as much as an inch.

The parade of mangled women surrounded the desk, but stopped, as if waiting. Waiting for one more.

Pam's heart felt on the verge of explosion. The doorway was open, but she couldn't see beyond it anymore. It was as if someone had put a black curtain over it.

A hand slithered from the darkness. Manicured nails curled around the doorframe, like a climber ascending a bluff.

Denise. Pam thought. The smell of *Joy Baccarat* and blood, flooded the room.

Denise stepped in. She was nude and quite dead. The knife protruded from her chest and on either side of it, rested flaps of skin. Mangled flaps of skin where her breasts used to be.

"Oh, Pammy," Denise said, stepping further into the room. "You were never beautiful and never will be." Denise looked at her with pity in her dead eyes. It was the way she always looked at Pam.

"No, fuck you!" Pam shrieked. "I am beautiful." She looked around the room at the disfigured women. The women whose lives she either ended or destroyed.

"Are you, though?" Denise asked.

Pam didn't feel anything, but she knew she had changed. A mirror appeared on the desk. Her shaking hands reached out to grab it. Her hands... looked old and wrinkled.

She stared at her reflection and almost vomited. She was herself again. Dry skin, pimples oozing, wrinkles, cold eyes, it was all back and then some.

"What the fuck?" Pam asked. She angled the mirror down towards her bare chest. That couldn't have changed. She would've felt her beautiful breasts deflate. No, they would still be perfect. But they weren't.

"No, no, no," Pam wept, staring at her sagging, veiny tits. She cradled her left one, like it was a dead puppy and wept. "You fucking cunts!" she screamed, looking at each of them in turn. "What did you do to me?"

Denise walked close, her legs at the front of the big desk. "Oh, Pammy, it's going to get worse. Much worse." She reached up with dead fingers and wrapped them around the handle of the knife. She pulled, slowly at first. The blade grated against her ribs, hissing as it was removed. Denise had a look of almost sexual pleasure on her face, her eyes locked with Pam's as she pulled harder.

"Ungh," Denise moaned. She quivered as the blade exited her flesh. "It's your turn now, Pammy." Denise smiled and licked her lips.

Pam stared at the gory blade as Denise tossed it on the desk. In a blink, the knife was in her hand and the mirror was gone. She smiled, knowing she'd use it to cut her way out. To slash and hack those around her and get back to Dr. DiBiro. He could fix her. He could fix anything.

Her fingers tightened on the handle and her knuckles cracked from the pressure. She tried to flex her hand, but the knife seemed to be a part of her, unrelenting.

Her free hand grabbed a breast. "No, god no!" Pam cried. Tears ran down her burned face, but she had no control. It was going to happen.

The edge of the knife was sharp and cold. She lifted her breast, setting the edge of the blade against her flesh. She was on autopilot, hell bent on self-mutilation.

"Please, not this. Anything but this," she begged. She began to cut.

The knife sliced through flesh and fat, like it was not even there. Blood ran down her stomach and the pain was almost electric.

"Fuck!" Pam yelled, as her first breast came off in her hand. She threw the useless flesh on the desk with a plop. The knife moved to her other hand, preparing to take her last vestige of womanhood from her.

The knife made short work of her second breast. Her entire body was in pain now, not just her mutilated chest. And then, she had a strange feeling. A feeling of rising, like she was coming out of a dream.

Deep in her subconscious, she was awakening.

It's only a dream, she thought in the moments between sleep and awakening. She was right, it was only a dream. A terrible, painful dream.

It was only a dream, but she would awaken to a nightmare.

Pam didn't open her eyes, but she knew she was awake. The pain, searing hot, let her know.

At first, she thought it to be remnants of the nightmare, but after a moment, she knew it was real. Her body lingered with a subtle paralysis from the dwindling anesthesia and her eyes fought to stay shut. Finally, after what felt like an eternity in burning darkness, she opened them.

Pam was still on the operating table, but she was covered with a sheet. It was cool to the touch, but she could feel the fabric sticking to open wounds. She also realized she was nude, not just topless. Stronger than that feeling of cotton was a taste. The taste of blood. Pam's brain was coming around and began firing all of its synapses.

Gently, Pam shifted her tongue, which was stuck to the roof of her mouth. She willed the muscle to move, to seek out the source of the coppery taste. Her eyelids fluttered, still thinking they were in the dream world. Pam's tongue probed...and found nothing.

Her teeth were gone! Well, mostly gone. Shards of discarded roots poked from some of the empty sockets, but most of them were vacant. Her body went into full alert mode, her eyes snapping wide, the thought of sleep no longer on her brain.

Pam heard a chuckle and realized Joe was sitting in a chair next to Denise's corpse, watching her. Slowly, she sat up.

"I figured the mouth would be your first find," he said, a cigarette in one hand and bottle of bourbon in the other. He put the cigarette in his mouth and pulled hard. The paper and tobacco crackled and glowed. He flicked the ash on the floor and sipped from the bottle. Joe wiped his mouth with the back of his hand. "It'll be the first of many." His old eyes, eyes that had seen so much, were ringed red with tears.

"What did you do to me?" Pam mumbled. Blood pooled in her mouth, filling the empty tooth sockets. She spat a thick rope of mucusy-blood onto the floor. Pain seemed to dance over her body, inflicting its fiery kiss as it moved.

Joe smiled, but it didn't reach his eyes. He took another, longer drag on his cigarette and tossed it on the floor. He ground it out.

"What did I do to you?" he asked with a laugh. "Well, I made you into what you are; a fucking monster." He drank, bourbon running down his chin. Joe tossed the bottle onto the floor. "I made you into a fucking mutant. A fucking ghoul. I made you into your true form."

Pam's mind was racing. Her senses were coming back in full force, but they felt *off*. She could hear, but even though he was only a few feet away, he sounded different. The smell of the smoke was there, but it was faint, like she had a stuffy nose…or no nose at all.

Pam's hands, now devoid of fingernails, shot to her face. Her nose, her near-perfect nose, was gone. A ragged, gory hole was left in its place.

"What the fuck?" she yelled.

Joe laughed again, this time in earnest. He squeezed his eyes shut, pushing tears down his stubbled face.

"I'm glad you found that before I have to leave." He looked towards the window. In the distance, the sounds of sirens pierced the night. "But it looks like my time is up." Joe picked up his cellphone, which had been face down on his lap. He showed the screen to Pam. 911 showed on the screen with a call timer running. "I called them not long ago. Just when you were starting to come to. I wanted enough time to witness some of your discovery, but I won't be here for the rest."

Pam shook her head, the pain amplifying with each motion. She couldn't help it; it was all to unbelievable.

"No, no, no," she muttered. Blood drooled from her mouth onto the sheet.

"Yes, Pam. Yes, this is fucking real. For once in my miserable life, I've created something real, not made of plastic or silicone. I've created a real-life fucking monster. But I guess it takes one to know one. It takes a beast to recognize another beast." He reached behind his back and pulled out the revolver. He stared at the oily darkness of the steel, turning the gun in the light. "You know, I could get a parole violation for having this," he said, smiling. "But, I'm a risk taker, that's for sure."

The sirens were getting closer.

Joe looked towards the window, knowing everything was coming to an end. "Well, my dear, I have to be going, but I'm sure I'll be seeing you soon." He smiled and put the short barrel into his open mouth.

Pam stared. She flinched when the hammer clicked back under his thumb.

The gunshot was deafening, even to her damaged ears. She jumped at the sound, but the sight was burned into her eyes.

The bullet entered Joe's soft palate, passing unobstructed through his sinus cavity. A tangerine-sized hole appeared at the top of his head, taking chunks of brain, scalp and bone with it. The ceiling was misted with droplets of blood and brain matter. Joe's nose and ears began to drip blood, slowly at first, but gravity helped draw the fluid out.

Pam watched the gun fall into his lap; a slight curl of smoke rising from the little barrel. The gunshot made her flinch, shocking her body with more pain.

Painfully, she threw the sheet from her torso and nearly vomited. Her body was carved. Her breasts—her sagging, pathetic breasts—were gone. Bare patches of flesh remained in their stead. Carefully she put her feet on the floor. The pressure in her heels sent shockwaves of agony through her damaged flesh.

"No, you fucker, no!" she yelled. More blood poured from her damaged mouth. Pam shambled over to Joe's corpse and grabbed it by the shirt collar. "No, fuck you!" she screamed in his face, the words jumbled and mushy. Blood speckled his already gory face, the new mixing with the old.

"What the fuck did you do to me?" She pushed him, but she didn't have enough strength to tip the chair.

Looking down at herself was more than enough, but she had to see. She had to know what he'd done to her. Pam braced herself as she stumbled to the small bathroom. It was dark, but she could see a full-length mirror shimmering. It called to her, beckoned her to gaze into it. To see what she truly was.

Pam lurched into the bathroom and stood in front of the dark mirror. Her fingertips were wet with blood; the empty nailbeds were bleeding in earnest. She found the switch and turned it on.

A monster stared back at her. A monster of flesh and blood.

Pam's face was destroyed. Her nose was two-pits of blood and bone. Snot and blood ran down to her lips to her toothless mouth. She was scalped. Not just shaved, but scalped. Her flesh had been peeled away, leaving only a wet skull behind. Finally, she figured out why her ears weren't working well; they were gone. Ragged holes and bits of flesh were the only thing left of them.

Her fingers gently probed at her damaged face and head.

"No," she moaned. Hot tears ran down her dry skin. "Fucking, no!" she screamed at the mirror, but the mirror wasn't done with her.

Her eyes dropped lower. Her tits, were gone. Both of them lopped off without ceremony. The flesh of her chest was carved. At first, she thought they were random lines, but her mind saw them for what they were: words.

Cunt, whore, bitch, crazy, monster. They all were dug deep into her skin. Each word cried blood down her torso, matting her thatch of pubic hair.

The sirens were close now, joined by the sound of tires squealing as they came to a halt outside of the building.

Pam touched the mirror, as if she could dispel her reflection like an image on water. She left bloody streaks on the glass and walked out.

The sound of heavy boots rushing up the stairs was in the back of her mind, but she didn't care. She was already dead.

Pam wandered over to Joe's corpse and stared. Even in death, he looked smug. Like he'd had the last laugh. Pam grabbed the gun from his cooling corpse and put the barrel to her skinless temple. She pulled the hammer back, feeling the smoothness as it clicked into place.

The boots were outside the door and she could hear voices. "Police, open the door!" They shouted, but Pam didn't care.

She took a deep breath, knowing this was the best way, the only way. She couldn't live as a monster, a beast that made kids cry. No, she was beautiful and if the world couldn't see that, then no one should. She closed her eyes and pulled the trigger.

Click.

Nothing happened. She pulled again and again. *Click, click, click.* It was like laughter and she could've sworn Joe was grinning at her. The gun was empty. The first five bullets were dumped into Bradley's body and the sixth had turned Joe's brain into pulp.

Pam cried and dropped the gun.

"Open the fucking door!" the police yelled. The heavy boots kicked at the old wood.

Pam's eyes, now full of tears, looked around for some kind of salvation. Something to usher her from this life. This life of ugliness. Then, she saw them.

Denise's implants were on the table. They were clean and pristine. Pam laughed and cried, walking over to pick them up. They were heavy and perfect in her hands.

The apartment door began to crack and pull away from the frame.

Pam collapsed on the floor, holding the implants against her mangled chest. They felt perfect, like they were meant for her. They made her feel beautiful.

The door shattered, flying into the apartment.

Pam watched the cops rush in, guns drawn. She welcomed them with a plastic grin.

About The Author

Daniel J. Volpe

Daniel J. Volpe is an author of extreme horror and splatterpunk. His love for horror started at a young age when his grandfather unwittingly rented him, "A Nightmare on Elm Street." Daniel has published with D&T publishing, Potter's Grove, The Evil Cookie Publishing, Death's Head Press and self-published. He can be found on Facebook @ Daniel Volpe, Instagram @ dj_volpe_horror and Twitter @DJVolpeHorror
Email@ DanielJVolpeHorror@gmail.com
Signed books and merch@ danieljvolpehorror.com

Billy Silver

Billy Silver, a low-life, self-downtrodden junkie, needs some cash to get his next fix. After getting kicked out of his own band, Shit Fist, losing his girlfriend, and left with no other options, he decides to sell his flesh to the ink of a needle at a newly opening tattoo shop.The mysterious artist, Talia, tattoos a cryptic design he's never seen.Shortly after getting inked, compulsions burn underneath his skin. His need to satisfy a newly arisen addiction to self-mutilation begins a descent into darker places than his miserable life never dared go.Eventually, violence against himself is no longer enough to satisfy his cravings. The urge to commit the grotesque brings his brutal tendencies to others... To strangers, to acquaintances, to his prostitute ex-girlfriend... When Billy finds out his band replaced him, with a new vocalist singing his lyrics on stage, Billy's desires reach their peak, and Talia, behind the fire of his rage, bears witness to all.

Awakened In Blood

After a drunken and adulterous night, Shane and Veronica's marriage is on the rocks. In an attempt to save their relationship, Veronica books a couple's retreat at an old lodge outside Ashmore, New York. Violent dreams, uncontrollable sexual desires and primal instincts haunt the guests at the old lodge. What is causing these bizarre urges? Will these savage imaginings become more than nightmares? As their stay at the retreat intensifies, will Veronica be able to save their relationship? Or will they succumb to the strange compulsions the house brings? Sometimes It's better to die than to be awakened in blood

Talia

In the early 1990s the rising popularity of the video cassette gave birth to a seedy, underground world of illicit pornography.
Talia, a Midwest dreamer, leaves home in search of fame under the blinding Broadway lights. But nothing could have prepared her for what she finds instead. Savage violence, bottomless depravity, and no way out.

Talia will unapologetically drag you into the foul underbelly of society. A sanity straining journey, full of hot bloodshed and betrayal

A Gift Of Death

A Gift of Death, is on tour. The three band members, Sarin, Vee-Exx, and Arsenic travel the country playing their dark brand of music for screaming fans. Their violent lyrics and goth style draw people to them. But, something else is drawing people to the mysterious trio...something sinister. They feed off the energy of the crowd, but desire something more: blood.

Cameron Snyder is an outcast. His love of death metal, extreme horror and his home life have left him on the fringes of high school society. When a prank goes too far, Cameron decides he's had enough. A relic of his dead father calls to him; a Colt 1911 handgun. He knows his life is not worth living, but can there be salvation? He then discovers a secret involving one of his favorite bands. A secret that could lead to immortality... or death.

Nestor and Cyril Visser run a private investigation business. A man shows up one day with a strange request, a deep knowledge of their past, and unlimited money. His request: find his son's killers and execute them. There's a catch though, he thinks the killers are vampires.

A Gift of Death combines heavy metal, revenge and

bloodshed galore.

Sew Sorry

YOU GET WHAT YOU EARN
Henry's mother has enough money to live more than comfortably. But the only comfort she can concentrate on is her bizarre obsession. She can't help but constantly seek out the donation bins on the darker side of the city. The only problem is, she isn't putting clothing into them, she's taking it out. Until one frigid night when she accidentally unveils her selfish secret to everyone. After the revelation, the layer of shame left lathered on Henry becomes backbreaking. As Halloween approaches, macabre ideas manifesting in Henry's head spark a series of events that will lead to sins far worse than stealing.

Garrison is hungry and cold. The only thing in his sights is finding a way to turn a dollar and his next foul meal. His own perseverance knows no bounds. His diabolical deeds are hidden in the shadowy alleys. He aims to survive, no matter who he has to trick or turn out in the process. But after burning too many bridges, he finds himself on an island. Alone, save for the salivating teeth of vengeance.

When a tarnished teenager and heartless hobo collide, the streets will run red. Rich or poor, we all rot the same.

Left To You

What would you do to save a loved one?
Robert's mother, Helen, is ravaged with cancer.
Every day could be her last, and Robert dreads losing
the last member of his family. Robert's friend
and Holocaust survivor, Josef, tells him an unholy story
and leaves him a way to save his dying mother.
But, as with everything in life, the salvation comes with a
steep price.
Will Robert accept what's left to him and save his
mother? Or will the cost be too high, weighing
Robert's soul down to the depths of Hell?

Visceral 2: Filleted Flesh

WARNING!

Consumption of these stories may cause vomiting, diarrhea, loss of sleep, impure thoughts, extreme anxiety, night terrors, suicidal ideations, hallucinations, and an increased risk of stroke and heart attack.

Basically, if you read these stories, you're doing so at your own risk.

Includes a foreword by Aron Beauregard, author of
The Slob and Modern Hysteria.

Only Psychos

Who will survive the storm?

It was a blizzard for the ages. Two, massive snow
storms strike back-to-back, causing
chaos in the Hudson Valley.

Anna, and her two children, are without power
and the temperature is plummeting. Their
situation seems bleak, but a break in the storm
gives them a chance at salvation. Anna flees her
home, hoping to find safety in a local hotel, but
what she finds is madness.

Scott is a man on the run. His travel partner, Mary,
is the quiet type, but that doesn't
bother Scott. The severed pinkie he keeps in his
pocket is all the distraction he needs.

Jackie and Beau, two young lovers, and budding
porn stars, have left their simple lives
for ones of adventure. On their wild trek across the
states, a blizzard puts a damper on their
plans, forcing them into an old hotel. An old hotel
with a violent and disturbing past.

The snow piles up and more guests continue to arrive…but who will see the morning?
Will the secrets in the basement remain hidden or will the years of torment be unleashed?

There are no normal guests at the Elk Dale Hotel…
Only Psychos!